Chicag

A Red Riley Adventure #1

Stephanie Andrews

Chicago Blue

A Red Riley Adventure #1

Copyright 2017 by Stephanie Andrews.

Published by Piscataqua Press

32 Daniel St. Portsmouth, NH 03801

Printed in the United States

www.andrewsauthor.com
join the newsletter, get good
karma and a free novella

The Red Riley Adventures

Chicago Blue
Diamond White
Solid Gold
Agent Orange
Deep Sea Green

The Levelers

The Grafton Heist
The Train Job

"Hold it right there, Mr. Fancy Pants!"

The call was just for a break-in, but the subject was listed as potentially armed and unstable. This guy looked neither, but I didn't want to take any chances. I thumbed the radio on my shoulder without ever taking my eyes off the man in front of me. "This is Riley. I have him on twenty-two. Request immediate backup."

"Listen—"

"Shut. UP!" I tried to make my voice deeper, front a little attitude so he'd stand still and keep his mouth shut. It wasn't unusual for suspects to not take me very seriously. Hell, I didn't take myself very seriously. I was a terrible cop and had no immediate plans to improve.

He was tall and good looking, and impeccably dressed, as if he had just dropped my entire paycheck on an entrée at Spiaggia.

Apparently, I convinced him that I wasn't in a listening mood because, with a slight shrug of his shoulders, he feinted to his left and then jumped to his right through the nearest doorway.

"Damn it!" I hollered and, without thinking, pushed through the door after him before it could close, before I could consider what an idiotic move that was.

It was a boardroom of excessive size, but the man had already made it to the other side of the room, on the far side of a huge cX5

onference table. He must have slid across the top of the table like Luke Duke. He wasn't more than fifteen feet from me, but I screamed at full volume anyway.

"Freeze! Show me your hands. *Now!*" My words echoed around the empty boardroom.

"My name is Carter Blalock," he said.

"Don't care."

Chicago Blue

"I'm the CEO of Illcom-"

"Don't..." Actually, that was really odd, since we were standing in the building owned by his largest competitor. A voice in the back of my head formed a question. Another voice, also in the back of my head, told me to stop asking questions. It also said my hair looked nice.

He raised his arms and the sleeves of his overcoat slid back, revealing a watch on his right wrist and a large, strange bracelet on his left. I say strange because it was metal, about four inches wide, and had a crystal embedded in it that was flashing a slow yellow light, like some sort of strange beacon. Seriously strange.

"I told Ralston to hurry, but it's too late," he said, his voice calm but his hands shaking. "It's not a bluff."

I had no idea who Ralston was. I only knew that I was sweeping floors 20 through 23, Jarvitz was doing 24 and 25, and Baker had the four floors below me. One of them would be here any minute. They'd cuff this guy while I kept my gun on him and then it would all be over and we'd all go have drinks until the adrenaline died down and I could go home to sleep.

With one hand, I kept my gun level and pointed at his chest, while with the other I pushed my hair out of my face. I was trying to grow out my bangs, but strands kept escaping their clips. My hair looked terrible.

"There's not much time," he told me matter-of-factly, and looked to his left, down the long table, toward the floor to ceiling windows at the end of the room. The drapes were open and from this height it was a spectacular view of Lake Michigan, even at night. Or especially at night. Whatever.

"We've got all the time in the world," I told him, "so let's just stay calm and we can work this thing out."

He looked at me with what seemed like pity, then glanced sideways at the flashing yellow light on his wrist.

Chicago Blue

"I'm trying to save your life," he said, and then turned and ran for the window.

It was one of those moments of clarity, when time slows down. I thought, "So he goes out the window. Less chance of a wrongful death suit. Not like I would be suspected of throwing a six foot, two-hundred-pound man through a window. The laws of physics being what they are, I'd have to be some sort of ninja assassin. A five-foot-six, freckled, red-headed ninja assassin. In ten years on the job I haven't fired my weapon once, why start now?"

Time sped back up to its normal rate and I watched him launch himself full force at the center pane. There was no sound of breaking glass, just the awful crunch of his nose breaking as he bounced face first off the reinforced glass and crumpled to the floor. That had to hurt.

I moved cautiously across the room, my weapon still trained on him, until I was within five feet. He groaned and rolled over. Blood was streaming from his nose onto his dress shirt. What kind of trouble was this guy in that he would try to leap out a twenty-story window instead of face a few years in jail? That shirt was totally ruined.

He opened his mouth to speak, but just then a small beep came from the bracelet on his wrist, and the yellow light turned to red and began to strobe faster.

Blalock looked up at me with eyes full of dread and resignation and through his bloodied lips came one word: "Run."

Maybe it was that look in his eyes, or the urgency of the blinking light, but I took him at his word. I turned on my heel and took two steps toward the door before I tripped over the plastic carpet protector and fell headfirst into the fancy high-backed chair at the head of the table. The chair rolled with my momentum, skidded and spun

3

Chicago Blue

halfway, dragging me around. Jarvitz's surprised face appeared in the doorway just as Blalock exploded. An enormous wave of force and sound struck the back of my chair, propelling me up into the air and then down, face first onto the solid, unforgiving oak of the boardroom table and beyond it into utter blackness.

I awoke in a bed that was clearly a hospital bed. The light was harsh and white. I blinked until I could see, more or less, and noticed my captain sitting in the chair next to my bed. He looked at me and shook his head.

"Red," he said, "you're alive."

He didn't sound that thrilled about it.

I closed my eyes and drifted away.

I could remember almost nothing of the explosion. Bits and pieces came back to me at strange times. I knew that both Jarvitz and Blalock were dead, but somehow I had survived with a concussion and a few other minor injuries.

The day I left the hospital was also the day of Jarvitz's funeral. I thought about going, but Cap just shook his head and looked at me like I had no sense.

"That," he said, "is a horrible idea."

So instead I went home to my apartment, where I found everything just where I had left it a week ago when I had gone out on my shift. I lived alone, no pets, no nearby relatives, so I don't know what I was expecting. Get well flowers, placed on the dining room table by a resourceful delivery person with a knack for picking locks? Casseroles outside my door? I felt nostalgic for the days of landline answering machines with the little red digital numbers telling you how many calls you had while you were out. My iPhone, which had not survived the blast, was telling no tales. I had talked to my mother, sort of, on the hospital phone, and my friend Ruby, so I don't really know who else would have called me. Maybe "The Guys"?

I dropped my keys in the dish on the little side table in the hall, then looked around my kitchen. The plants needed water. A lonely ant made his way across the kitchen counter, dragging a crumb. There were a few dirty dishes in the sink, but luckily none had sprouted any mold. Yet.

In my bedroom, I eased slowly out of my coat and looked at myself in the mirror above my dresser. Besides the purple bruises that still showed around my eyes, and the shaved area of my head above my right ear—twenty-seven stiches—I looked pretty normal. My nose was still

Chicago Blue

the Riley Special, but it seemed to point slightly to the left now in a way that it hadn't before the accident. The incident? The ... Oh hell.

I was captivated by my reflection, my injuries made me look remarkable and scary. Usually, I was amazingly mundane. My hair was naturally red. Freckles punctuated my pale skin. I got chosen for plainclothes work a lot because I could spend all day walking through a mall or a college campus and no one would ever look twice at me. I had a pretty good body, because I worked hard not to be one of those cops that can barely get out of the cruiser without help. I was medium height, with medium breasts, medium ass. Medium, medium, medium. The Guys never asked me out because, they said, I was "one of The Guys," and that would be weird. Though it never stopped them hitting on Amanda Arsenault. Or Vicky in forensics.

Well, if I was one of the guys, why hadn't any of them come to see me in the hospital? I know. Jarvitz. I get it. Somehow it was my fault for not warning him the room was about to explode. I was just feeling sorry for myself.

I looked around the bedroom and felt depressed. Apart from a framed Art Institute poster, which I still loved, everything in here seemed a decade old, and stale. Old CDs stacked next to my stereo: Green Day, Moby, Gwen Stefani, Destiny's Child. I didn't buy CDs anymore, of course, I just downloaded tracks, but my taste hadn't changed much. In my closet, jeans, chinos, t-shirts, blouses in muted colors. In some ways, I felt that after my dad died, after I joined the force, I just stopped seeking out new things, new experiences, and life became a grind.

Did I mention I was feeling sorry for myself? I did? Okay.

I changed, slowly and stiffly, into my red one-piece bathing suit and then eased into some sweats and took a

Chicago Blue

towel from the closet. My apartment building had an indoor pool, and swimming was my preferred way to work out. Since I could barely walk, I figured a leisurely float might be just the thing.

And it was. I returned to my apartment after an hour in the pool, and took a long, hot shower. Feeling much better, I dressed in gym shorts and my Veruca Salt t-shirt, then sat at the dining room table to sort through a week's worth of mail. Most of it was junk, but then I came across an envelope with the departmental letterhead on it. Curious, I opened it right away.

What the...? Suspended? By mail? What a bunch of assholes. It looked as if I had been suspended for sixty days while the incident of April 26th was being investigated. With half pay. I was required to stay in Chicago during those two months, as I would be required to be available to answer questions concerning the explosion when the board needed me to. I would be required to check in with my captain once a week. Three requireds in one paragraph. Don't they own a thesaurus?

I have to admit, I was tired of being a cop. I had probably considered quitting at least once a week for the last three years. That said, it still stung to be unceremoniously dealt with by mail.

I picked up my new phone and called Ruby.

"Who is this?!" She said immediately, suspicion and annoyance mixing into her Czech accent. Ruby had lived in the U.S. since she was six, but still managed to talk as if she had just arrived.

"Ruby, it's me, Kay."

"This is not your number."

"It is now, new phone."

"You can keep your old number, you know, just because you have a new phone you don't need a new number."

9

Chicago Blue

"But my old phone was an iPhone, and my new phone is one of these other things."

"Doesn't matter."

"Yes, well, that's not why I'm calling. I'm calling because what the hell?"

"Are you in pain?"

"No." I sighed and pinched the bridge of my nose, but that just made little shooting pains run through my skull. I looked at the hosta that sat in a big pot below the window. It looked like I felt, thought it would only take a little water to perk the plant back up. Those things are impossible to kill, which is why my apartment was full of them. "Well yes, a bit, but that's not what I mean. I mean I'm totally suspended."

"I know, that was a week ago."

"I only just got to my mail."

"They told you by mail?" Ruby snorted. "That is very lame, no?"

"Yes. Ruby, what's going on?"

Ruby Martynek was a former beat cop who now worked in the administrative offices. After a few years on the force she had severely damaged her knee and opted for a desk job. She was one of my few friends in the department, or anywhere really, and she had a great nose for news. All the important stuff came across her desk, and she managed to absorb it all without ever seeming to be nosy.

"This Blalock, he was a big time guy, head of Illcom."

"Then what the hell was he doing in the Farnham Building? Aren't they sworn enemies? Some sort of corporate espionage?"

"Nobody knows. And they blame you for that."

"What? That's nuts. It's not like I exploded him. Or caused him to explode. Or whatever."

"Yes, but now there is no one left to answer any questions."

"But *I* didn't explode him!"

"Plus Jarvitz."

"Right." I fell silent.

"Listen, honey. None of this was your fault. It will all get straightened out. You'll see. Meantime, enjoy your vacation, relax, recover."

"It's not a vacation, it's a suspension!"

"Potato, potahtoh."

"Let me know anything you hear, okay?"

"Tomato, tomahtoh."

"Uh huh. I'm hanging up."

"*Na shledanou.*"

"Goodbye."

4

Carter Blalock. Seemed I had some time on my hands, so I thought I'd look into Carter Blalock. A normal person might take a double dose of their prescribed painkillers and lay on the couch watching *Titanic*, again, but I was too stirred up by the suspension. I couldn't relax, and I had questions that I wanted answered.

I can't say that I had ever really loved being a cop. For some people, it's a way of life. They'd rather be in their cruiser than anywhere else in the world, and most of them were doing the job for all the right reasons. I sort of fell into it, and never quite climbed out. Certainly, other things called to me. I had wanted to be a lawyer, I had expected to be a lawyer, but that hadn't worked out. I also liked art, and history, and reading.

Two things kept me on the force. One, admittedly, was inertia. I was still young enough to get my law degree. I could probably get some decent financial aid to make that happen, but every time I got serious about it, something pulled me back, and I lost my momentum. The other thing was my strong sense of justice. I hate, *hate*, to see people getting away with things. At the same time, I hate to see people getting a raw deal because they don't have the education or the money to properly defend themselves. Being a beat cop let me play mediator. If I thought someone needed a second chance, I could look the other way. If I thought someone was taking advantage, I didn't mind stepping in and making things a little more difficult for them. These scenarios play out daily when you are patrolling a city like Chicago.

Lately, however, the rise in shootings, though not in my part of the city, was giving me pause. Add to that a feeling that the higher-ups in the department didn't necessarily have my back, and I was seriously thinking once again of quitting. In fact, just a few weeks ago I had gone once more to Northwestern to pick up enrollment information.

All that said, however, the suspension rankled. I might want to quit, but I wasn't going to do it under a cloud. It seemed the worst sort of expediency to decide that my behavior was suspect simply because I had failed to stop the explosion. I wanted to get to the bottom of this.

I threw my laptop in my satchel and took the bus downtown to The Creamery, my favorite coffee place. It had lots of old, mismatched furniture and served coffee in miscellaneous mugs collected over the years. I didn't like the new ultra-modern places, with stainless steel, or even copper tabletops and overly artful lighting. I had been getting my coffee there every morning for about six months when one day a few weeks ago I just said, "The Usual." The barista—baristo?—was a tall black guy named Oren who worked most every morning, and he gave me a look that indicated that he had *no* idea who I was or what my regular drink was. It was depressing, but par for the course. I thought about changing coffee shops, but I knew it wasn't his fault.

Oren was there today and I ordered a large dark roast with cream only. I found a table in one corner and pulled out my laptop. I fired it up, grimacing at the Chicago Police logo that always came up first thing. When I entered my password I was greeted with an error message: *user name or password is incorrect*. I typed it again, and then again to make sure I hadn't made an error. After the third time the message read: *Security lockout, please contact system administrator.*

Damn it, when they said suspended, they really meant it. I was completely locked out. I couldn't even get to a browser to log into the coffee shop's wifi. I pulled out my phone to use instead, but it had a tiny screen, and by the

Chicago Blue

time I found my way to Google my head was already splitting. I took off the Cubs hat I was wearing to massage my temple, but instantly felt self-conscious about my shaved head and the white gauze bandages. The remnants of two black eyes was off-putting enough, I didn't want to scare everyone.

I put the cap back on and took out my medicine bottle, looking around furtively at the other patrons to see if anyone was watching the crazy woman taking drugs. I thumbed two tablets into my mouth and washed them down with a gulp of molten lava that scalded my throat. Damn, they brew it hot here. I wondered briefly if they would let me back into the hospital if I asked nicely, because things out here were just not going well.

I decided to go to the library and get on the computers there, but when I stood up I felt a bit dizzy. Suddenly, the idea of going to the library every time I needed the internet seemed too much of a struggle; I needed another solution. I sat back down and finished my coffee.

Twenty minutes later I left The Creamery feeling marginally better. The drugs must have kicked in. I also had a new idea: Marty. I fished around in my satchel, looking for his business card. The bag was an old leather one Dad had given me when I went to college, and I still used it every day when I wasn't on duty. It looked like the kind of bag an important old barrister would carry as he entered the courtroom, and this wasn't by accident. Nothing my dad did was ever by accident. I hadn't cleaned it out since I got it, more than a decade ago, and now I started cursing as I stuck my fingers in all the various interior pockets. One had something sticky in it, but luckily the next pocket had old Kleenex in it, which I used to wipe my fingers off. Finally, I found a little stash of business cards that I had collected from random

Chicago Blue

people over the years. I searched through them until I found one for Martin Martynek. "Technology Acquired, Inc." Marty had once told me that he could get any kind of computer or phone I needed, if I ever needed one, and fast. At the time I had wondered: Why would I ever need one fast? But today seemed like the day. The address was only a few blocks away. I was surprised by the Lake Shore Drive address, as it seemed a little upscale for Ruby's nephew, but I decided to head that way. It made sense to get my own laptop, but if it was only going to be for a few weeks then I didn't want to spend a lot of money. If it turned out to be longer, I could always trade up.

I walked along the lake. It was spring in Chicago, a city that was known for always being too hot, or too cold, but today was a Goldilocks day, and I enjoyed the cool breeze and the sunshine.

I breathed deeply and relaxed, until suddenly sirens split the air a block or two away. That was part of Chicago, too, the noise and the mayhem. I craned my head to the right and could see black smoke rising behind a few of the skyscrapers. There was a fire, or something going on, but I was suspended, so screw that. I lightened my step and whistled as I strolled along the lake. Whatever that was, it was somebody else's problem.

I turned onto the block of the office building that was listed on the card. It was fancy and about thirty stories tall. This couldn't be right. I'd only met Marty a few times, at Ruby's place, and not only was he too young to have an office in a place like this, he was way too uncouth, unwashed, uneducated, un-everything. Don't get me wrong, he was very bright, but in a relaxed, laid-back way that certainly didn't fit in with this neighborhood. I leaned against a tall lamppost made of black aluminum, looked again at the card, and reached for my phone—it made sense to give a call first.

Chicago Blue

As I was dialing I heard a strange metallic "ping" sound above my head, and felt a tremor pass from the light pole to my shoulder. I looked up, expecting I don't know what, when there was a ricochet sound by my feet and a sharp pain in my lower left calf. Ouch, damn it. Just then a wasp buzzed by my ear and my drugged-up brain finally made the connection. Someone was shooting at me.

This seemed ridiculously unlikely. Cop shows and news hyperbole aside, there isn't a huge amount of gunplay on the streets of Chicago in broad daylight, and especially not on Lake Shore Drive. So, I did the foolish thing. I stood there and looked around. When I noticed an SUV with tinted windows, idling half a block away, I suddenly got a creeping feeling all over my flesh. It was so unquestionable, so visceral, that I knew I was in real danger. I doubled over and puked my coffee everywhere, perhaps saving my own life as I heard another bullet ping off the lamppost where my head had just been. I looked up to see that the SUV had lurched out of its parking spot and was speeding toward me.

Without thinking, I sprinted up the walkway to the glass entrance of the building, all the aches and pains of my injuries forgotten. I heard a screech of tires as the SUV jumped the curb and started after me. A man exiting the doorway looked up in surprise, and then terror, and then leapt away to the side. I ran through the door as it was swinging shut and heard the squeal of brakes behind me. I hunched my shoulders, waiting for the shattering of glass, either from bullets or from the vehicle smashing into the front of the building, but it didn't come. Without looking back, I ran for the place ahead that seemed safest: a solid wooden door to the right of the elevators. I burst through it and into a stairwell, with so much momentum that I couldn't stop, and ran straight into the

17

Chicago Blue

metal railing, knocking the wind out of myself. I turned to
see the door close behind me, but when I stepped
toward it the world tilted and then went dark.

5

When I woke up my head was a cracked churchbell. I was lying flat in bed, looking up at a movie poster of Olivia Newton John and Travolta—no wait, that's Michelle Pfeiffer, must be *Grease II*—where the hell was I? I turned my head to see a wall covered with movie posters, all from the 1980s. Seriously, where the hell?

I sat up, slowly, and pulled the blanket off me, only then realizing I was in my underwear. Jesus Christ! I jumped back under the covers in a panic. A secret government prison wouldn't feature a poster of *Blade Runner*, would it? How about a crazed serial killer? More plausible, though surely a psychotic madman wouldn't have left my underpants on, would they?

The room was clean and simple. Besides the movie posters, there was the bed, a chest of drawers, and a bedside table with a lamp. A clock on the table read 11:00, but I didn't know if that was AM or PM, because there were no windows.

Just then a door opened. I clutched the blanket up to my chest as a young man entered.

"Oh good, you're up. I was about to call an ambulance."

"Marty?"

"Yes, that's right. You're Kay, right? Ruby's friend?"

"Where the hell are my clothes!!"

"In the bathroom, you had puked all over them. I washed them in the sink. It was pretty gross."

"Shut up. Stop."

"Are yo—"

"Just. Stop. Back up. How did I get here?"

Marty took a step back and raised his arms in a gesture of surrender. He was in his early twenties, and unshaven. He wore jeans, a hooded sweatshirt, dark

Chicago Blue

framed hipster glasses, and had bare feet. He didn't look particularly threatening, but I was completely freaked out.

"I was working at my desk when I heard loud noises," he began. "Squealing tires maybe, or some sort of accident. I came out in the hall and up the stairs to see what was going on and found you lying on the landing covered in puke—and bleeding."

My hand went instinctively to my head but only felt dry bandages.

"I put a new bandage on," Marty said, "and one on your calf."

I reached under the covers and felt, sure enough, some sort of gauze taped over the back of my left calf. I had no idea why I would be bleeding there, but then again I was a bit lost at the moment.

"Thank you," I said calmly, but my brain was screaming. "Could I get my clothes please?"

"I'm sorry, they're soaking wet. You've only been asleep about 45 minutes."

"How about something else, then? Do you have something I can borrow? Because I am about to completely lose my shit."

Marty pointed at a dresser in the corner. "Help yourself," he said. "I'll be in the other room."

His entire wardrobe seemed to be made up of jeans and sweatshirts, and a few minutes later we were standing in his living room looking like twins, or an ad for Old Navy.

I felt so much better being dressed, even if the clothes were baggy on me. I don't think I had ever thought of myself as particularly shy, but I hate to think of myself as weak, and it's hard to feel strong when you are half naked, and not by choice. My nerves were shot, and my mind was still going to a thousand different places, but as I stood there, barefoot on the gray industrial carpet, I managed to take several deep and calming breaths, like I had learned in taekwondo class a million years ago.

The room had a kitchenette and a small work area that was mostly taken up by two six-foot folding tables acting as a computer workstation. There were three monitors, and many small boxes with flashing lights, well beyond my skill level, and of course cables running everywhere. To the right of the table was a floor to ceiling corkboard covered with slips of paper, tacked up photos of computer equipment, and a poster of Michael J. Fox climbing out of a DeLorean. Marty saw it catch my eye.

"That's a great one, huh. Hello, McFly!!" He reached out to rap his knuckles on my head but thought better of it, either remembering the big bandage on my skull or just from basic manners, I'm not sure which. He gave a halfhearted knock on his own head. "A classic."

"Surely," I agreed, with the slow nod one saves for the less lucid citizens one encounters on a cop's daily beat. "Can we?"

"Right. Right!" He exclaimed and gestured to the bar separating the kitchen from the rest of the room. I gingerly climbed up on one of the barstools while he got me a glass of water and leaned on the other side of the counter.

"Okay," I began. "You said you came up the stairs. Are we in the basement?"

"Yes, it's uh, my artist's studio."

"With no windows..."

"Not all artists use paint, you know. Technology is where the front edge—"

I held up a hand to stop him midsentence. "Sorry, headache too big." I hated to be rude, but a longwinded explanation of the deep artistic aspects of computer coding was not what I was up for just then.

Chicago Blue

"Right. *Right!*" He had a way of emphasizing the second "Right" as if he had just suddenly understood an incredible mystery, thanks to you. His eyes widened and his eyebrows shot up. It was a little adorable. He rummaged through some of the kitchen drawers until he came up with a bottle of aspirin, which he handed to me.

"We're in the basement, in my brainstorming bunker, as I like to call it. I have a little house in Evanston, but when I'm working on a project I like to come here so I can focus, and also remain anonymous."

I was shocked.

"You have a house?? I thought you just fixed old computers. Last time I saw you at Ruby's I swear you asked her for twenty dollars."

He looked away sheepishly.

"That was a long time ago. A year, maybe? Things change quickly in my industry. I'm working on some very exciting game applications, and some other things as well." He looked to the side again as he spoke. He was a terrible liar—or I'm an excellent cop—but I let it go for the moment.

"Are you hungry?" he asked, and I realized I was. When I nodded, he pulled out some eggs and cheese and started to make an omelet. "What are you doing here, in this building?"

"I was looking for you, actually," I said and he turned around with alarm. I pointed to my leather bag, which I had spotted in the corner with my shoes. "My laptop is frozen and I was hoping to either have you fix it or to pick up a used one for me to use while I'm on suspension."

He sighed in relief.

"Oh yes, I heard about that, I'm sorry. Throw it up here on the counter and let me take a look at it."

Chicago Blue

"I should call Ruby," I said, "and let her know I'm here."

He looked at me again and his brow crinkled. "I'm not sure that's a good idea," he said, and as he attempted to turn the omelet it became clear I would be having scrambled eggs.

"Oh?" I asked, raising my eyebrows. I could see he was trying to judge just how much to tell me. He knew I was a cop, after all.

"It's just, well, the excitement upstairs earlier. After I carried you down here, I went back up to the lobby and looked around. A lot of guys in dark suits. They didn't see me, and I think it is better that they didn't. And better if Aunt Ruby doesn't know anything about it."

"They were after *me*," I told him in a flat voice.

"What?"

"Whatever you're into, you don't have to worry about *those* guys, they were after me. I stopped outside to call you before knocking on your door, and someone in a black SUV with tinted windows started shooting at me."

"You're kidding me!! Why?"

"I don't know. It's got to have something to do with Carter Blalock."

"The CEO who blew up all over you?"

"Well put," I grimaced and swallowed two aspirin. It had to be connected to Blalock, my attempt to apprehend him, and the subsequent explosion. There was not a single other thing in my life that would cause someone to take interest in me, never mind try to kill me. My run-in with the telecom CEO was the only thing unusual that had happened to me in...I don't know, a decade?

He slid the eggs onto a plate and set them in front of me. As I dug in—I was ravenous—he moved my laptop

Chicago Blue

to his worktable and plugged it in to something. The screen lit up and things began to beep.

He came back over to the kitchen, took two glasses from a cabinet, and poured us both some orange juice. "So you don't think this had anything to do with me?" he asked.

"No, it doesn't, but you clearly thought it did."

"Well, there's a lot of balls up in the air right now."

"Marty..." I gave him my big sister stare. He was cute, but a decade younger than me. Flirting was unlikely to work. If I was going to get any help from him it was clearly going to require playing up my friendship with Ruby.

"And you're a cop," he continued.

"Not right now, I'm not."

"True. Still, we don't know each other very well. I think it's best to stay on subject."

He carried his juice over to the laptop when it made a new and different beep.

"Here we go!" he said, and started typing on the keyboard. I swiveled on the barstool, but couldn't see the computer screen, only his lit face, which moved slowly from delighted, to concerned, to aghast.

"What is it?" I could feel panic rising in my throat.

He looked at my bag in the corner. "Is your cell phone in there?"

"No, why? I mean, I dropped it on the sidewalk when the shooting started. It's probably smashed."

"Good," he said grimly as he crossed the floor and took each of my upper arms tightly in his hands.

"What the hell?" I tried to pull away.

"Good," he repeated. "Then nobody knows you're here," he said and dragged me off the barstool.

At first I thought that he meant something sinister, and he was going to either kill me and eat me or keep me in this basement in a cage. Neither of which was very appealing. But that wasn't it.

"Look at this!" Marty exclaimed, pulling me urgently across the room. I realized he didn't actually mean me any harm; he was just freaked out.

He pulled me to the screen of my laptop, which was showing a video of a local news report. On the screen, I could see a downtown skyscraper, and, as I watched, a fiery explosion blew out one of the upper floor windows, sending glass and debris raining down to the street below. This image was replaced by a newscaster, and Marty hit the volume button as the woman began to talk.

Emergency crews are still arriving on the horrific scene here at IllCom Tower, where we have confirmed at least one person severely injured from an upper-story explosion. The building is currently being evacuated. After last week's bombing at the Farnham Building, the tech world is understandably on edge.

"Oh my god!" I gasped, but Marty shushed me.

"Wait for it..." I looked back at the screen, where the action had shifted to a man behind a desk in a newsroom.

Police have not released the name of the bombing victim yet, but they are circulating this photo of a person of interest in the crime.

"Oh...no..." I croaked as my police ID photo came up on the screen, with my name beneath it.

Suspended police officer Kay Riley is sought as a suspect in today's bombing. She was last seen in the Lake View area, and viewers with information on her whereabouts are urged to call the hotline number at the

Chicago Blue

bottom of your screen. While police have refused to articulate Riley's involvement, it should be assumed that she is potentially armed and dangerous.

I sat down heavily in his office chair, staring at the screen. Marty reached forward and muted the sound, and then looked at me.

"I don't..." I said. "That's not..." and then I started to heave up the eggs I had just eaten.

"No!" shouted Marty. "No no no no!" And he spun my chair away from the computers and toward the trash can in the corner. And just in time, too.

"Honey, I'm home!"

Marty put his bags down on the counter and looked around the bunker. "Kay?"

He found me in front of the bathroom mirror, slowly peeling the bandage away from my skull. The stitches underneath were creepy looking, the skin around them puckered and yellow.

I examined the wound, then looked at the bags under my eyes. It had been three days since I arrived in the basement and, while my bruises were looking much better, my already pale skin was starting to look ashen. I looked like a ghoul. "I have to get out of here," I thought to myself.

"I have it all taken care of," chimed Marty, as if he had read my mind. In his hand he had a razor and a package of bright red hair dye.

"I thought I said a wig!"

"Trust me, this is better. More comfortable, too." He set the box of dye on the sink and edged his way behind me. The bathroom was tiny but brightly lit, with small white and green checked tiles. Technically, this place was an office and not an apartment, so there was no shower or tub. Another reason I needed to get out of here— washing yourself in the sink gets old, real quick.

Marty picked up a brush and used it to part my hair on the side with the stiches. It felt weirdly intimate. I think I might have actually blushed, which was foolish.

It had been a weird three days. Obviously, I had tried to leave at first. I didn't want Marty to get in trouble when they found me. He would be arrested for sure. But he was adamant that I stay, and honestly, where would I go? After much discussion, we decided to include Ruby in the loop. Of course, she had been frantic when I had disappeared and then turned up on the news as one of Chicago's most wanted. To their credit, neither Marty nor Ruby ever once asked me if I was actually involved in some criminal undertaking.

It was decided that I would stay here for a few days, but the place was tiny and Marty and I were constantly in each other's space. To make matters worse, I couldn't go outside, so he was forced to do errands for me. I'd sat down with paper and pencil and made a list: Bra size, panty size, favorite toothpaste, favorite shampoo, brand of tampons. I honestly couldn't remember when I had last shared such intimate details with a man. I mean, I'd been on dates in the past year, some that ended up in one bedroom or another, but asking a man to buy you Playtex Sport Tampons with Flex-Fit Technology was a whole other level.

Marty turned on the electric razor and got down to business, trimming all the hair off one side of my head, down to about an eighth of an inch.

"Woah!" I exclaimed, raising my hand to stop him.

"Shh. Trust me!"

"Did you just shush me?" I grimaced, but lowered my hand and gripped the sink. I had come to realize over the last few days that I was way, way out of my depth. Marty was no criminal mastermind, but he wasn't bogged down by all the bureaucratic nonsense that I had lived with day to day for the last decade. Being a cop meant following orders. It meant routine. You did the job, and you did it exactly as you were trained to do it. I had been itching to break out of that mold, but becoming a fugitive from justice hadn't been what I had in mind. It was hard to get out of that law enforcement mindset, and that mindset only showed me one resolution to this problem: turning myself in. And I didn't see how that could possibly end well.

Chicago Blue

"I can't believe I'm having my hair done by someone who looks like he hasn't combed his own hair in a month."

"That's on purpose," said Marty. The hurt look on his face only lasted a moment before being replaced by a lively smile behind his scruffy, five-day beard. "It's the style! Now hold still..."

8

Later that day I was walking across the campus of Wilbur Wright College, led by Marty, who was talking nonstop in his animated way. Sometimes he reminded me strongly of a Muppet. A Muppet with serious computer skills.

"It's not very famous, but there's lots of good tech going on here, and more importantly, I happen to have a key to an empty student apartment. It will be perfect!"

I followed him past the campus buildings to a ring of apartment buildings surrounding a swimming pool. Nobody was in the pool, it was still only April, but there were some students lounging outside, looking at their laptops or even reading an actual textbook. Made of actual paper.

I was wearing a pair of ragged jeans tucked into Doc Marten boots, and a leather jacket over a black t-shirt. My hair was shaved tight on both sides, but a long swoop of magenta fell over to the right, hiding my stiches and falling in my face every three seconds. I had to admit, Marty was absolutely right: nobody would ever find me here, dressed like this, looking like a student. I was still in the city but miles from my precinct. It was perfect, for now.

We entered one of the buildings and climbed the stairs to a door on the second floor. Marty pulled some keys from his pocket and let us into a miniscule studio apartment. Just looking around made me feel old. This was probably somebody's idea of freedom—away from Mom and Dad, future ahead of them. It made my moderately sized one bedroom look like a palace.

"Who's place is this?" I asked. It obviously belonged to a woman, because it was orderly and there was even a box of tissues on the table beside the sofa/bed. However, there were also three computers set up on a worktable, a bookcase full of mass market sci-fi paperbacks, and what appeared to be a real broadsword leaning in the corner. I walked over and ran my finger along the blade of the sword. It was amazingly sharp.

"It belongs to an acquaintance of mine. We met at a gaming conference last year. She's crazy good at Vainglory."

"And where is she now?"

"Brazil, all semester." He handed me the key, which I put into my jeans pocket while I took a quick look around. On the counter Marty laid a student ID with the name Margot Parker. No picture. "This will get you into the library, where you can use the computers. Probably better if you don't use these," he added, gesturing at the computers in the room.

Just then someone knocked on the door to the apartment. I gave an involuntary yelp and then clamped my hand to my mouth, looking around for a place to hide, but Marty was nonchalantly opening the door.

It was Ruby.

She stumped in, supporting herself with a black wooden cane, and set a bag of groceries on the counter, along with her oversized handbag.

"Did I hear someone scream?"

"No," I stammered. "Just caught me a little off-guard."

"You are one to talk, Miss Fugitive From Justice!" she exclaimed in her Czech accent. She limped into the room and looked around. "Not much to write home about, eh?"

"It's perfect. I'll be safe here. Marty did a fantastic job."

Marty beamed, setting down another bag of groceries.

"Better than he did on your head!"

Marty scowled. "It's all part of the plan, Auntie. She looks just like a college student."

"That hair! So red! It will attract unwanted attention."

Chicago Blue

"No," insisted Marty. "Just the opposite. She looks nothing like Kay Riley."

Ruby gave up arguing, and sat down heavily on the sofa. "Right, to business. Martin, my handbag."

He brought the bag to her and she plopped it on the floor with a thunk, unzipped it and drew out a manila folder. She was only in her early fifties, but Ruby always acted as if moving through the day was a struggle, with many exasperated sighs and a lot of huffing. Maybe she picked up these habits during her long and painful knee rehabilitation and never lost them. Anyway, she always reminded me of a cranky grandmother, though you will *never* hear me say that out loud. The fact was that she was here to help, with no questions asked, and what that meant to me, I can't put in to words.

"As you probably know," Ruby began, "this second explosion, the one at Illcom, it nearly killed Arthur Vincente. He's in hospital, very critical." She handed me a photo of Vincente, likely from the company website. He was an older black man with Desmond Tutu hair and glasses.

"He's chair of the board," Ruby continued. "He took over as CEO after Blalock blew up in your face. It is of course suspected that Mr. Farnham is retaliating for the earlier bomb, but the whole thing is crazy, a bit too James Bond for real life. This other board member, Frances something, saved Vincente's life somehow—they haven't given out too many details. As you might expect, the cops have been crawling all over the Farnham Building all week, but they are starting to wind things up. Not finding any of the smoking guns, as you say."

Ruby paused for breath and looked again around the little apartment, her eyebrows rising as she noticed the sword. "I really think you should turn yourself in. This is craziness."

Chicago Blue

"I know, Ruby. I really know it's crazy, but why am I a suspect? I know I was in the same room with Blalock, but it's not like I went there with a bomb. It's all a blur, I really only remember a few little bits, and then waking up in the hospital. And I wasn't anywhere near Illcom when this second bomb went off. What if someone on the force is trying to frame me?"

Ruby gave a dismissive grunt.

"Too much drama. Dirty cops, they steal some evidence, they shake down some drug dealers. They don't mastermind frameups on the fly after a high-profile bombing. Trust me, I know cops."

"Still, I'm going to lay low for a while and see what I can find out. Plus, I've already changed my hairstyle."

"Is that what you call that?" Ruby pushed herself to her feet, and handed me the manila folder. "I had a feeling you would say that." She reached into her voluminous handbag and removed a small press pot and pound of ground coffee.

"Oh, Ruby," I grinned, "you're the best."

She looked around the tiny kitchen. "Is there even a tea kettle?"

"There's a microwave," I assured her, "this is great."

Ruby looked at the microwave and shuttered with disdain. She reached into her bag again, and pulled out a white envelope.

"What's this?"

"Some cash," she said, waving off my objection. "Until you can get things straightened out." She tapped her finger on the manila folder, which was lying on the countertop. "Here's everything I could scrape up on the Farnham case. I won't be able to get my hands on anything about Illcom for a couple days." She made her way to the door. "Martin," she said imperiously. "I don't approve of you being involved in this."

Chicago Blue

"But—" Marty broke in.

"But," Ruby continued, "it's better than that shady thing with the Bitcoin."

"That wasn't shady, Auntie!" Marty drew himself up indignantly. "That was an excellent business opportunity, and you made your investment back, plus twenty percent."

They continued arguing out the door and down the hall. I swung the door shut behind them and threw the deadbolt. I moved to the kitchenette and started to put the groceries in the tiny fridge.

What a strange world, I thought to myself. Two weeks ago I'm normal old Kay Riley, today I'm a wanted fugitive.

And tomorrow? Tomorrow I become a private investigator. A private investigator with only one case. I should get business cards anyway. 'Cause I've always wanted them.

9

A deep, uncontrollable shudder ran through me as I stood in the elevator of the Farnham Building, my finger hovering over the button for the 24th floor. Two buttons down was 22, where less than two weeks ago two men died. I took a couple deep breaths. *Get a grip, Riley!*

I got a grip and pushed the button for 24, smoothing my skirt and looking at myself in the mirrored wall. I'd rearranged my hair to cover the stitches, and perched a little straw hat on my head to tone down the red coloring and hopefully block my image on the security cameras. I looked ridiculous—nobody wears hats. Maybe a Cubs hat, but it didn't seem to go with the rest of the image: blue skirt, blue blazer, shiny black shoes, all acquired from the Goodwill on Washington Boulevard. Hell, I should have a wicker basket in the crook of my elbow, filled with petunias.

I had started singing, "There's a bright golden haze on the meadow," the only line I know from *Oklahoma*, when the elevator stopped on the 14th floor and the door opened.

"There's a bri... oh, hi," I chirped to the man who walked briskly on. "Which fl—" I started to ask, in my friendliest Becky voice (I'd decided my name was definitely Becky. I was a total Becky), but he had punched the button for the 22nd floor before I got it out, then turned his back to me to watch the floor numbers light up as the car transported us higher and higher.

He was a powerfully built man with a bald head and cauliflower ears. He had a neatly trimmed beard and mustache with just a bit of gray in it. His suit was also gray, with thin white stripes, and he wore a silvery blue tie accessorized with a Bluetooth earpiece. His skin was a deep bluish black. He wasn't talking, but the light on the earpiece kept flickering, making me think he might be listening to someone talk. Turned out I was right.

"Okay," he said, in a soft, deep voice. "I'm nearly there. Tell Mr. Farnham to meet me... No, in 2215, the other suite is still being worked on." He had a beautiful voice, with a touch of dour seriousness that made you hope to never hear him raise it in anger. He was clearly ex-military, or ex-linebacker, maybe ex-husband. The kind of good-looking dangerous that indicated he maybe didn't have a lot of wholesome arts and crafts hobbies.

The elevator opened on 22, and he stepped off without ever a word or look of acknowledgement. This is exactly what you want when you're undercover, though I couldn't help feel slighted. It was always the same with me: I don't want to be judged for my looks, unless the judge is giving high marks. It's one of those things I know I shouldn't worry about, yet it's always in mind. You'd think becoming a police officer would dispel all those feelings of inadequacy, but it was just the opposite. Most of my colleagues were men, bigger than me and oozing bravado, at least on the outside.

Through the closing elevator doors I could see construction workers in the hall, milling about. It was probably a big job to fix the damage that Carter Blalock had done.

At the 24th floor, I got off the elevator, took a drink from the water fountain in the plushly appointed hall, and then entered the nearby stairwell. I didn't want to enter the 25th floor, the executive and top floor, via the elevator.

I had decided to start the investigation by looking into Farnham, just like the cops had done, to find out why Blalock would target him, and if Farnham was the type of guy to bomb someone in retaliation. And yes, the police seemed to be abandoning this line of inquiry, but I wasn't the police anymore, so clearly I was now smarter than the police. Or at least less hemmed in by so-called "rules" and "laws." Impersonating a Becky, hacking into the Farnham computer system, these kind of tactics would have been frowned upon on the force. To be clear, *Marty* was trying to hack into Farnham, but on my behalf. My computer skills were not great, to say the least. Not that Marty had succeeded, not yet, but he was likely to. In the meantime, I had done a little research on my own over the past week.

Everyone knows that Illcom and Farnham are the Apple and Android of the telecommunications world—natural rivals—but it's been that way for at least a decade. So what happened recently that would make one of them bring death and destruction on the other?

My research on Ferris Farnham showed him to be a wunderkind in his late forties who never really got over years of Bueller jokes in high school. An overachiever on every level, he not only developed cutting-edge communication software, he was a yoga master and sat on the board of a humanitarian nonprofit he helped found. I assumed he sat on the board in the lotus position. In video clips of interviews, he struck me as one of those people who, just below his liberal veneer, was seething with rage and hubris.

Farnham and Blalock had actually known each other back in graduate school, at Northwestern, which is why it was no coincidence that both businesses are headquartered in Chicago rather than in Silicon Valley or New York. I was beginning to think that whatever had happened between them, it was maybe a personal war more than a business one. Why would Carter Blalock sacrifice his life over a business squabble? Why not hire some muscle to do it, unless you were deeply, personally

Chicago Blue

involved? Unless you want to see it done with your own eyes to satisfy a personal vendetta.

Hmm. Maybe. All I knew as I climbed the stairs to the 25th floor was that something about this whole situation was not quite right. I was missing something obvious, forgetting some crucial fact, and I couldn't put my finger on it. It made my head hurt.

Outside the door to the top floor I took a minute to compose myself and work through my plan. I jogged quickly up and down the last five steps until I was a little out of breath. Then I straightened the stupid straw hat on my head and barged through the door.

"Oh, dear!" I said breathlessly, with just a hint of stagger in my step as I walked across the lobby to the reception desk. I held one hand to my chest and fanned my face with the other. The receptionist rose to her feet, unhappy with the interruption but also clearly concerned.

"Are you okay?" she asked me. Her reading glasses swung from a chain around her neck. I love that. You just don't see that anymore.

"I'm sorry," I gasped, in my best Becky voice. "I got turned around in the stairwell and sort of panicked. I was coming to pick my boyfriend up, he's a construction foreman, but I couldn't find him, and then the fire, and well I ju—"

"What fire?"

"—st didn't know what to do, so I headed for the—"

"What fire!" the woman interrupted again.

"There's a big fire where my boyfriend is rebuilding the office that was bombed." I suddenly widened my eyes in terror. "You don't think there's another bomb, do you?"

The receptionist glanced quickly to her left, where large mahogany double doors stood shut. "Mr. Farnham's down there!" she blurted with rising panic. Ignoring me completely, she stepped around me and ran out the door to the stairs.

Nicely done, Becky!

I scoped the room quickly. It was beautiful and elegant, with the receptionist's desk square in the middle, likely made of hand-harvested rainforest bamboo, or something like that. One wall was covered in windows, the other two walls, facing each other, each featured heavy-looking double doors and expensive-looking art. None of the doors were labeled, but the receptionist had given me the clue I needed, and I sprinted for the door she had glanced at.

I slipped through the unlocked door and clicked it quietly shut behind me. The only light was from the late afternoon sun coming through the floor-to-ceiling windows. In addition to a large, clean desk, there was a conference table with half a dozen Herman Miller chairs around it. Bookshelves lined one wall, most filled with books, but some with pictures and various awards or mementos. The facing wall held three large, and I mean large, flat screens, maybe for video conferencing or maybe he was really into to playing Vainglory.

My attention was caught by a printed three panel Japanese screen in the corner. Behind it I found a small Buddha statue, a prayer rug, and other shriney-type things that I didn't understand. Interesting, but not what I was after.

What *was* I after? Well, who knows? Wasn't this the part of the movie where some important detail was supposed to jump out at the main character? I examined the pictures on the shelf, in case one of them was of Ferris and the Unabomber. I looked through the desk drawers but found nothing unusual. The top of the desk held only a lamp, a keyboard, and a mouse. When I

Chicago Blue

touched the keyboard, one of the widescreens on the wall leapt to life, showing some spreadsheets.

I was trying to make heads or tails of it when I heard voices in the lobby. Well, this was going to be awkward. I quickly hit the Escape button on the keyboard, but not much happened. I sprinted to the screen on the wall, looking for an off button, but there wasn't one. On the other side of the door, the voices grew louder. I stared helplessly at the bright flat panel, paralyzed by panic, then ran behind the Japanese screen just as the door to the office opened.

Carefully, deliberately, I controlled my breathing, then moved my head slowly until I could see through the thin slit between the hinged panels.

Farnham was standing at his desk, frowning up at the lit TV screen, likely trying to remember if he had left it on or not. He wore a loose-fitting gray suit with a black turtleneck. He was taller than I expected him to be from his pictures. The setting sun glinted off his wire-rimmed glasses as he swept his gaze around the room.

Just as he turned toward my hiding place a low buzzing attracted his attention. He reached into his inside suit pocket and pulled out his phone, holding it up to the side of his head as he turned around to gaze out at the setting sun.

"No. Nothing up here...Nothing? Greg, this can't be a coincidence. Someone is messing with us... You're the head of security, you should understand what another bomb going off in this building would do to this company. Not physically, but to the stock price. We are all going to pay if it happens again, whether anyone else is hurt or not." Farnham slapped his hand on the window pane in frustration, and I had a quick flashback to Carter Blalock trying to jump through a similar window three floors down.

Chicago Blue

Farnham had lowered his tone: "You're right... I'm sorry, Greg, but this is really getting to me. They came at me pretty hard about the Illcom bomb. Arthur was hurt badly, I hear, maybe Aldo as well... If you know anything, if you find out *anything*... No, I don't suspect you, of course not, but you know more of what's going on in this building than anyone, and Carter called *you*... Valerie?... No, I haven't seen her all week... Well, I assumed because she was shaken up by this whole thing... In fact, I'm meeting her for early lunch at eleven tomorrow at The Drake and I have a few pointed questions for her... No, I don't really think... Well, I mean I know that, but I have to consider all possibilities!"

From my research on Farnham I knew that Valerie must refer to Valerie Archer, Farnham's second in command. I guessed the other office, off reception, belonged to her. This could be interesting. It seemed there wasn't a lot of trust at the highest level of Farnham Enterprises.

Farnham was still on the phone as he walked past me and out the door.

"No, I'm on my way now. I sent Janice home for the day, it was almost six anyway... I'll stop in on my way down..."

And he was gone. Wow. I didn't have to look down to know my hands were shaking. I could feel sweat running down my spine. This was too much; I was out of my league. I was used to beat work, domestic calls, and the occasional parade. Still, my first operation as a freelance spy, and I hadn't blown it. Yet. I relaxed my body the best I could, and then began to concentrate on how to get out of there undiscovered.

Just as I was about to move from behind the screen, a scraping noise above my head startled me. I huddled back down behind the screen as, incredibly, the ceiling panel directly above Farnham's desk slid open to reveal a dark hole above! Out of that hole a woman lowered herself until she was hanging from her hands, at which point she dropped silently onto the surface of his desk in an alert crouch.

I clapped my hand over my mouth to keep from exclaiming, as the woman swept her eyes around the room to make sure she was unobserved. She was wearing a white catsuit. Honestly! Made out of Lycra, I think. Certainly something that stretched, because it fit her body tighter than...I don't know. Really tight. Tight enough for it to be obvious that she was in incredible shape. Olympic gymnast kind of shape. Yes, I could drop down out of the ceiling onto somebody's desk, but it wouldn't look anything like what she just did.

She dismounted, equally silently, from the desktop and moved to some filing cabinets that ran underneath the monitors along the wall. A few moments of searching, and she removed a single piece of paper, folded it, and slipped it into the sleeve of her left wrist. She closed the drawer and then remounted the desk. Her long brown hair flowed out behind her in a ponytail. The sun had finally set, but in the soft glowing light I could see that she had a beautiful, youthful face, round and luminous. With a flex of her incredible leg muscles, she leapt straight up, her hands grasping a water pipe up in the ceiling. She pulled her knees up to her chest, and then inserted her feet through the hole, inverting her whole body so that the last I saw of her was her ponytail, disappearing into the blackness.

The ceiling tile slid shut, and I exhaled for the first time in maybe five minutes. I listened for sounds of her leaving through the ceiling, but I heard nothing. Not a scrape, not a sound.

Chicago Blue

Holy crap, what had just happened? Did I mention that I was completely out of my league?

Com. Plete. Ly.

10

I sat in the little park behind The Drake hotel, twisting the long black braids of my wig. I also wore a white oxford shirt with a skinny black tie and black pants. Comfortable black shoes.

Three hours earlier I had come up with this plan while working out at one of the Wilbur Wright rec rooms. I would have preferred to swim, but I didn't have a swimsuit and was too lazy to put on a disguise to go buy one. Instead I rode a stationary bike, my mind spinning along with my legs. It felt good to work up a sweat. Ideally, cops should be in top physical shape, but that wasn't always the case, and I had slacked a bit in my regimen. I'm sure seeing the cat burglar the day before, with her lean, perfect body, might have had something to do with it, too.

As I sweated and planned my next step, I watched the news and weather scrolling by on a screen mounted high on the opposite wall. Nothing about me, but after about half an hour I was startled to see a familiar face as they began a piece on the funeral of Carter Blalock.

The deceased had been a good-looking guy in his forties, with a full head of blond hair that needed a trim. In the clip they showed, he was standing at the St. Patrick's Day Parade with his dark-haired wife Belinda and a young daughter, maybe eight years old, holding a glittering green shamrock on a stick.

The next clip was from two days ago, and showed the widow and daughter leaving the funeral and getting into a long black car with tinted windows.

I felt bad for them. Whatever Blalock was into, and it was surely something bad, his wife probably knew nothing about it. Certainly, the kid didn't. It's always the kids that have to deal, for decades sometimes, with the shortcomings and misfortunes of their parents. When you have kids, every mistake you make ripples down through generations. Man.

I stopped cycling and took a long drink of water, going over everything I knew about the case.

Who was I kidding? I only had one lead: 11 AM. Lunch. The Drake.

That's how I found my bewigged self crossing East Lake Shore and circling around to the front of The Drake, entering through the revolving door. As I found the Coq D'or (seriously) Lounge it was 11:35 PM, still early for lunch. The place was nearly deserted. I grabbed a full water pitcher from the busing station and made my way through the room. All the real wait staff were huddled near the bar, looking intently at their phones, occasionally casting a furtive glance toward their tables.

Farnham was sitting at a small table in the far corner, dressed in jeans and a black turtleneck. A small amount of styling gel in his hair was the only hint that the look was calculated. He was forking the remains of an absurdly expensive salad into his mouth, talking at the same time.

Across the table from him sat the woman who had to be Valerie Archer. I had seen her in the newspaper a few times. As someone who was young, black, and female, she stood out as a high-ranking executive, and the media loved her. She was slim, with a long neck and very close-cropped hair, unstraightened. Her well-tailored cream business suit contrasted with onyx jewelry and black strappy shoes. She was a very well put together woman, but today she had an expression on her face that was half anxiety and half anger. I moved closer until I could hear them.

"Greg Ralston told you that?"

"No," said Farnham. "Janice told me that."

Chicago Blue

"I'm not surprised. She could have done a bit more digging before jumping to conclusions." She glared at Farnham with a fire in her eyes. "I *did* meet with Aldo Frances, because I'm trying to get to the bottom of this! It's been two weeks, and we still have no idea who's targeting us. We need to stop pointing fingers. Don't you realize this is likely some third party targeting both Illcom *and* us? Aldo is in charge over there now, and Arthur Vincente was nearly killed."

"Yes, but we didn't—"

"Have anything to do with that, I know. But look, Ferris: Carter Blalock, Arthur Vincente, and Aldo Frances. That's Illcom three, Farnham zero. You can't blame the police for thinking we were involved. You can't blame anyone for that. It's already affecting our stock price."

"You don't have to remind me," Farnham cut in. "I'm getting constant calls from both coasts." He set his fork on his plate and looked around the dining room for the waitress, presumably for his check, but she was nowhere to be seen. I ducked my head and straightened the silverware on a nearby table. "But Val, if it was someone else, then what the hell was Carter doing in our building when the bomb went off?"

Archer frowned. "That's what's really bugging me, too. It doesn't make any sense at all." She stared off into the distance for a minute, then snapped out of it and looked at her watch. "I've got to go," she exclaimed, reaching into a small purse that matched her shoes and jewelry.

I was standing stock still a few tables away, lost in thought. Something Valerie Archer had said made me think of something, something from the night of the explosion. Pieces were falling into place...

"You! Spacegirl!" I jerked my head toward the voice to see Archer waving her arm at me. I shuffled over, keeping my head down, a pitcher of water in one hand.

49

Chicago Blue

"Yes, ma'am?"

"Where on earth is our waitress? It's like she fell off the edge of the earth." Her voice was calm, and she seemed more bemused then angry, but the frustration was still simmering below the surface. She seemed like someone who didn't often lose their cool. Under normal circumstances, she was probably a very nice person, and her position as Vice President at the company indicated that she was clearly driven, and brilliant.

"I'm not sure, ma'am. Would you like me to take that for you?"

"Yes please," she sighed, handing me the card.

I headed for the hostess station, turning at the last moment toward the bathrooms and then down a long hall to the rest of the hotel.

Like I said, she was probably a very nice person, which is why I felt a bit bad as I headed out the revolving door and onto the street, her Platinum Mastercard snug in my pants pocket.

11

I ran a few errands, and then went back to my "safe house." Safe dorm? Whatever. I removed the wig, strangely happy to have my crazy red hair back, and washed the makeup from my face. I took a hot shower and put on some of Marty's loaner clothes: some comfortable sweats and a t-shirt. It was only about 7 PM, but I was going to make an early night of it. The adrenaline from my lunchtime escapade had worn off, and I felt exhausted. When you're in the middle of it, the rush is enormous, but when it's gone you're left completely drained. You would think I'd felt this a few times while on the force but honestly, I had never been in a single high-speed car chase, never mind a shootout. Never delivered a baby in the back seat of a car, never talked a jumper off a ledge. Nope, I had pretty much spent ten years arresting drunks and vagrants. Occasionally, some piece of crap who had beaten his wife. I'd had more excitement in the last six days than in the last six years on the job. I honestly was not missing being a police officer. At all.

I examined the stitches on my scalp in the mirror. No sign of infection. In the medicine cabinet, I found some fresh Band-Aids for the gash on my calf. I probably should have gotten a few stitches there, but it seemed to be closing up on its own pretty well. I had to remember to thank Marty for doing such a nice job with the first aid.

I ambled out to the living area where the black wig was now perched on the hilt of the broadsword, past the counter that divided the tiny room from the tiny kitchen. I stretched languidly and reached for a plastic bowl from the cupboard and filled it with cereal and milk. I turned to sit at the counter, but the countertop was still covered

Chicago Blue

with shopping bags, so I walked back into the living area, flopped down on the sofa, and turned on the TV.

I was soon sound asleep with the cereal only half finished and Jerry Taft on the screen, telling me the weather tomorrow would be sunny and crisp...

I was back in my uniform, back in the Farnham Building, gun drawn and looking for an intruder. "Criminal" by Fiona Apple was playing loudly through overhead speakers, and I was wearing very heavy boots that were a few sizes too large for me—it made it very difficult for me to walk, every step was a struggle, and sweat was pouring down my forehead and stinging my eyes. Nevertheless, I struggled toward the boardroom door, which was just ahead of me. I knew I was supposed to be in there, but it was taking me forever to get there.

Inside the boardroom, a shirtless Carter Blalock greeted me warmly, walking across the thick carpet toward me. He held a green shamrock on a stick.

"Glad to see you here!" he exclaimed with real affection. "Sorry about my attire, it's just so hot in here with the fire and all."

"Fire?"

He stretched out his hand to shake mine. "Yes, the fire, from the explosion."

I looked down at his outstretched hand, recoiling when I saw the bracelet strapped around his wrist, blinking brightly with an amber light.

"Don't be afraid," he told me, but then the light on the device turned red, there was a heavy, repeated banging noise, and I screamed.

I lurched up from the sofa, sending my cereal bowl flying to the rug. Milk splattered everywhere. My t-shirt was drenched with sweat, and drool was coating one side of my mouth and even on to my neck.

Chicago Blue

Bang! Bang, bang! Someone hammered on the door. Oh good Christ, I thought I was having a seizure, but then I took a deep breath and the room came back into focus. I wiped my mouth on the shoulder of my shirt and looked for my service weapon, before realizing it was still back in my apartment, my real apartment, on the other side of the city.

I took a step toward the door, crunching some Frosted Flakes under my bare foot. Damn. I kept quiet, tiptoed to the door, and looked through the peephole into the gray hallway of the apartment building.

It was Ruby, cane raised, ready to pound on the door a third time. I let her in quickly, looking up and down the hall, but there was no one else around.

"What's wrong with you, Kay?" Ruby bustled in, her black bag over her shoulder. "You didn't answer the door, I was worried about you, you know?"

"I was asleep, I'm sorry." I stepped around Ruby to pick up the bowl and the bits of cereal and put them in the sink. "This dream, Ruby, I remember—"

"It's only 8 PM, you were already asleep? I think this suspension is making you lazy."

"I'll have you know, I had a very exciting day—"

"What's all this?" Ruby interrupted me, waving her arm at the shopping bags as she stepped around the wet spot on the carpet and placed her bag on the sofa. "You shouldn't be out shopping, with your face all over the news!"

"Oh," I answered evasively. "I needed some new clothes. I wore a disguise the whole time, and certainly the police wouldn't be looking for me in the shopping district. I don't want to wear Marty's jeans and sweatshirts forever, and I still don't dare go to my apartment."

"Right, but Vuitton? J. Toor? You can't afford this stuff with no income!"

Chicago Blue

"Yes... well, that's a long story," I stuttered. I was suddenly feeling a bit self-conscious about my shopping spree on Valerie Archer's credit card. I had really been embracing my criminal fugitive persona; it was strangely freeing to feel like all the rules had been abandoned, all the niceties and courtesies gone. When I wore the wig and the glasses, I really felt like somebody else. Yet there was a nagging guilt, my old self still there, hands on her hips and tapping her foot, looking at me like Mom used to look at me when I came in past midnight.

Anyway, I had then ditched the card, so I wouldn't get carried away, or tracked for that matter. I threw it in a rain gutter. Right after I bought a few additional items at the Army Navy Surplus on Lincoln.

Ruby had started rooting through the shopping bags.

"Holy Mary!" she exclaimed, pulling out a pair of black leather pants. I blushed. I had been thinking of the Lycra-clad catwoman when I bought those pants (I didn't think I could pull off Lycra, but the black leather looked pretty damn good on me). They seemed like something a superspy should wear.

"Never mind that," I said, pulling Ruby away from the counter and over to the sofa. "Let's just say I had a little help from an anonymous benefactor. And besides," I added with a little pout, "I really needed something to improve my mood. This has been such a nightmare."

"I'm sure," said Ruby, and put her arm around me, pulling me close. That was why I loved her. "I'm sure it has been," she went on, "but there's an old Czech saying: When you find yourself in a hole, first stop the digging."

"I don't think that's Czech," I frowned at her.

"Of course it is Czech!"

"Never mind," I said, sitting up straight again. "I almost forgot the thing I forgot!! I'm so glad you're here."

I jumped to my feet and paced.

Chicago Blue

"I had this crazy dream just now, but right in the middle of it I remembered something from the explosion. Something important!"

Now Ruby was all ears.

"What? What was it?"

"When I saw Carter Blalock, just before the explosion, he wasn't carrying a bomb. He was *wearing* it!"

"Like a suicide vest?"

"NO! No, no no, it was a bracelet. How could I have forgotten?"

"Well, head trauma, of course," said Ruby, "but a bracelet? Are you sure it wasn't just the dream?"

"No, it really happened." The moment I said it out loud, I was more sure than ever. "It was big, like a Wonder Woman bracelet. Maybe it was just the detonator, I don't know. It had a yellow blinking light on it. Blalock freaked out, tried to jump out the window, and then told me to run just as the light on the bracelet turned red."

I was nearly jumping up and down I was so excited by these recovered memories, but Ruby was frowning.

"What is it?

"Well, this means we've been all wrong."

I stopped bouncing.

"About what?"

"Well, motive of course. We assumed that Carter Blalock was trying to plant a bomb in the Farnham Building when the police showed up. But..."

"He *was* the bomb!!" I interrupted. "Somebody was *using* him as a bomb!"

12

The next day, Aldo Frances exited the elevator on the executive floor of the Illcom building. He looked around the clerical pool, looked right at me without noticing me. He did seem a bit nervous, and a bit suspicious, but his eyes passed right over me without pausing or showing any sign of alarm. My disguise seemed to be succeeding.

My cubicle was on the main aisle, so he walked very close to me on the way to his office, which was at the far end of the building, adjacent to what had, until recently, been Carter Blalock's office. Frances was the head of new product development, so his real office was on one of the lower floors where the engineers were hard at work on the next big thing in fiber optics or whatever. He probably was uncomfortable to also find himself the CEO. Arthur Vincente had become interim CEO after the first explosion killed Blalock, but then the second explosion sent him to the ICU, leaving Frances, as the senior officer, suddenly in charge. He was the Gerald Ford of the telecom industry. No, I wasn't alive when that happened. But I've read some history books, I'll have you know.

The report had been that Frances had also been critically injured in the second blast, but this turned out not to be true. He seemed perfectly fine. Sometimes the news gets it wrong.

I had been in this cubicle for about an hour. According to the unprotected Gmail account on this desktop computer, the desk belonged to Angie Delacroix, who ordered a lot of clothes from Land's End and had 452 Facebook friends.

Only one person had said a word to me the entire time: a cheerful woman with spiky blonde hair asked how long I was temping for, and wasn't it a shame about Angie.

Chicago Blue

It was, it was a terrible shame, I agreed, though I had no idea what had happened to Angie.

I had come here because Aldo Frances, like me, had survived a bombing, presumably perpetrated by the same individual. Had he seen something, anything that would give me a clue to go on?

I gave Frances enough time to get settled in at his office before I got up and made my way over to visit. I was wearing an embroidered Louis Vuitton shirt and matching skirt that was several levels above my office temp pay grade, but it seemed unlikely Aldo Frances would know much about fashion, and I had been dying to try it on. Strappy black shoes with a very low heel (so sensible!) completed my businesswoman attire. I was wearing purple-framed reading glasses with zero magnification that I picked up at a Jewel Osco. They went great with my intense red hair. I wore a bright, dangly earring on the ear that was showing, and nothing on the ear that was obscured by my swoop of hair. It was a case of hiding in plain sight. Clearly my temp job was a hold over until my acting career took off, or my ultra-modern paintings took off, or whatever hip thing I did when I wasn't at Angie's desk.

I held a sheaf of blank copy paper in one hand as I rapped lightly on Frances's door and let myself in. Aldo Frances looked up as I entered, pulling off his reading glasses so that he could see across the room.

He was about 65 years old, with a big head of salt and pepper hair, a strong face and a closely shaven chin. When he walked past me I was struck by how short he was, maybe five foot five. He didn't look much like a scientist. In his blue suit, well-made but not very stylish, he looked like an insurance executive from the 1950s. To him, I must have looked like some sort of punk rock alien, because his eyes widened as I crossed the floor to stand right in front of his desk.

"Yes, what is it?" he asked briskly.

I set the sheaf of papers on his desk, then reached over to the back of his telephone console and unplugged the cord.

"Hey! What on Earth..." He stood quickly. "Who are you?"

I put my finger to my lips and motioned him back into his seat. Amazingly, he was intimidated by the strange move and actually sat back down. I sat in one of the two chairs on my side of his large desk.

"Mr. Frances," I began, removing my glasses. "I don't actually work here, but I have some important questions to ask you. I'm afraid they're quite urgent."

He sat up alertly in his chair. "I thought you looked new—I would have noticed the hair—but the girls out there change all the time. Are you a reporter?"

The girls. Lovely, old man, lovely.

"No, I'm not a reporter. I'm guessing you've had enough of them. I'm an investigator."

"I've already talked to the police, at great length. If you're with an insurance company you need to talk with Arthur or Carter's lawyers. Honestly, I'm having a difficult enough time just keeping the company going day to day. This is not my world—I'm usually down in the lab. I don't really see how I can help you." He ran himself out and sat looking at me, probably wondering how to get me out of his office. He looked to the closed door, but made no move.

"I can't reveal my employer, I'm afraid," I said conspiratorially, leaning toward him and talking in a hushed tone, "but needless to say, there is a lot at stake here, and we can't be completely sure that you're not still in danger."

Chicago Blue

He didn't like my secrecy shtick, apparently, because he rose from his seat, looked at his disabled phone, and then started to come around the end of the desk. Damn, well, here we go...

"Mr. Frances, wait. My name is Kay Riley, I'm a—"

"Police officer!" he broke in, the name registering with him, because of course it would. He'd been told I tried to kill him. I stepped between him and the door.

"Wait," I pleaded, bracing my stance as best as I could in my well-tailored skirt, ready to stop him if he made a run for it. My aim was to look formidable but not threatening.

"I am *not* involved in this," I pressed on. "I know it sounds ridiculous, but someone is setting me up. I didn't know why until just recently."

He tried to sidle slowly to one side, but I adjusted to keep myself between him and the door. I was about an inch taller than him, even in the low shoes. He eyed the door, but he hadn't started shouting his head off yet, so there was still hope. I could see that behind his eyes there was some serious thinking going on. Option weighing. I had to connect quickly.

"The bracelet," I blurted, and I saw his eyes widen. "They are framing me because I know about the bracelet. I saw it on Carter Blalock. You know what I'm talking about, don't you?"

He took a step back, slipping his hand in his pocket, and drawing out a cell phone. Of course he had a cell phone! What was I thinking? Still, he hadn't tried to make a call yet. Maybe he was worried I would jump him if he did.

"You could know about the bracelets because you could be the one who put them on us."

"All right, that's true. But I didn't! I'm just a Chicago cop. I answered a call about a break-in." I was getting frustrated. "I was just standing there doing my job when that bracelet flashed yellow. Blalock looked at me with such fear, like I've never seen. And then he tried to jump out the window."

I may have sobbed a little at this point, because Frances lowered his phone and looked at me with an odd expression on his face.

"He tried to save me, told me to run," I said, looking directly in his eyes. "And now somebody's trying to kill me, and I need to know what the hell is going on..." I looked at him helplessly.

He sighed and moved back behind his desk, sitting down and motioning me back to the chair I had been in.

"How much do you know?"

"Not much," I admitted. "Everyone thinks this is about a Farnham/Illcom rivalry, but if Carter Blalock was forced somehow, maybe with threats to his family, to be in that building, wearing that weird detonator, then it seems likely that some third party is trying to pit you against each other." I sighed. "And because I saw the evidence, I've been made a scapegoat. Which tells me that someone in the police department is in on it. I don't know how else they would be able to accuse me with such authority."

Aldo leaned forward. We were compatriots now, both survivors, so I had decided to call him Aldo. It's a great name; I'd never met an Aldo before.

"Well, I can fill in some of the holes for you, but not all, I'm afraid." He got up and paced the room, a man used to working and thinking on his feet. "On that terrible night, I got a call from Carter. He sounded crazed, insane. He was saying something about Belinda and Gracie, when suddenly there was the sound of a struggle and then Greg Ralston came on the line."

Chicago Blue

"Wait, the security guy? How did you know it was him?"

"I've known Greg a long time. He's been with Ferris forever, and I worked for Farnham when he first started."

I must have looked startled, because he continued. "I know, it's all a bit intertwined, which is part of why I agree with your assessment. It must be an outside party. Ferris and Carter were much, much closer friends than anyone in the public knew. They wanted it kept quiet, for many reasons.

"Anyway, Greg told me that a secretary working late had heard noises, and seen someone sneaking through the building. She called 911, they called Greg and sent you, I suppose. Greg got there first. He found Carter nearly delirious with panic, saying over and over again to get away from him, because he was a bomb. Greg pulled the phone away from him and, when he realized it was me on the other end, he asked me what was going on. Of course, I had no idea, but when he described the bracelet Carter was wearing, I told him that yes, it was completely possible that a high-powered bomb could be that small. When Greg hung up, he told Carter what I had said, and Carter turned and fled. Greg ran after him, but went downstairs, figuring Carter was trying to get to the street. Evidently Carter had gone upstairs instead."

Wow! That all seemed to fit. Carter was a bomb, and somebody had tried to blow up both Carter and Farnham at the same time. Killing two birds with one of the birds.

"There's more," Aldo said, moving to the computer and tapping a few keys. "I don't think it's the police that have set you up. Look."

He rotated the monitor until it faced me.

"This is from our security footage." He tapped a button.

Chicago Blue

The video showed somebody walking down a long hallway, then walking through the cubicle garden just outside the office we were now in. It was a woman, in a police uniform. She had reddish brown hair hanging down from a cap that covered most of her face. She was carrying a black doctor's bag in one hand. She entered the door to the office next to this one and disappeared inside. Aldo stopped the video.

"That's you," he said, "the same night that Arthur and I were nearly killed."

"It is not!" I protested.

At that moment, there was a knock on the door. I jumped half out of my skin, but Aldo sat quickly in his chair, tossed me a pen, and pointed at the papers I had left on his desk.

"Come in," he called as I scrambled to grab the pen and take on the appearance of somebody writing down the instructions their boss was dictating.

It was Perky Spiky Hair.

"Mr. Frances, you wanted me to remind you about your 10:40 appointment with Accounting. It's on the fifth floor, so you want to give yourself some time to get down there."

"Thank you, Tina—"

"Tracey."

"Sorry, Tracey. I'll be done with..."

"Carlotta," I offered.

"...Carlotta in about five minutes, and I'll head down." Tracey left.

"Ugh," Aldo moaned. "Accountants. Maybe it would have been better to be blown up." He instantly caught himself. "I don't mean that, of course. A terrible thing to say. Carter gone, Arthur in the hospital."

"What happened to you and Arthur?"

Chicago Blue

"I'll try to give you the short version, but it was the most terrifying fifteen minutes of my entire life. I still relive it when I close my eyes." He stood up again, and moved to look out the windows. "It was after business hours. Arthur and I were in his office—which had recently been Carter's office. Arthur is retired, but as the president of the board we all thought it best if he became the interim CEO. Anyway, for the last several evenings we had met to discuss issues and have a drink together. On this night, shortly after our first drink, we both passed out. There must have been something in the scotch. An hour later, according to the security cameras, someone dressed as you came in and put one of those exploding bracelets on each of us."

"Did you see who might have entered the office to spike your drink?"

"No, I'm afraid the security cameras aren't on during business hours, only at night, so it could have been anybody."

"But that anybody must have been familiar enough with Illcom to know that about the video cameras."

"Or they got lucky."

"No," I persisted. "They knew about the video cameras, because they took the precaution of wearing a disguise when they entered in the evening. They knew I had been at the earlier explosion, and people would think it was me when they saw the hair and the uniform."

"Hmm. You may be right. But how does that help us? You being here now proves that it's incredibly easy for anyone to act like they work here. There are so many employees, always coming and going."

"You probably want to beef up your security."

"Of course, you are absolutely right about that."

"What happened next?"

Chicago Blue

"Right," he said. "We woke up and it was morning. We both had a bracelet locked on our wrist. Each had a solid green light embedded in it. From my conversation with Greg, I knew we were in great danger. Arthur ran for the stairs; the main reception area is one floor down. I had noticed a small data jack on the bracelet, and I ran to my office to get a cable and plug it into my computer.

"It was a fairly simple mechanism, once you were connected to the software. I heard Arthur's voice on the intercom, telling everyone to evacuate the building—he had run to reception to try and save lives.

"With a little more fiddling on the computer my bracelet popped open, but just then the light started blinking yellow. I found the command to disarm the bracelet, and the light went off completely."

"Oh my god!" I gasped. I was breathless and on the edge of my seat.

"I grabbed my laptop and the cable and sprinted down to reception where Arthur was still trying to clear the building. His bracelet was blinking yellow. I plugged it in and had just gotten it off his wrist when the light turned red. Arthur grabbed it in his right hand and threw it across the room, but it only flew about ten feet before it exploded. Arthur was directly between it and me, and the force blew him back into me and knocked us both to the ground."

"Wow."

"He shielded me, inadvertently. He must also have called 911 when he first reached reception because suddenly there were firemen everywhere. They pulled Arthur off me and I didn't see him again until the hospital. I didn't have a scratch on me, but Arthur has some severe burns and seems to be in a coma. I think he hit his head pretty hard against the desk or the floor. He hasn't woken up."

Chicago Blue

We sat there in silence for a minute, until Aldo shook himself back to the present.

"I've got to go downstairs, and you've got to get out of here."

"What do we do?" I asked, helplessly, feeling overwhelmed.

Aldo reached into his pocket and gave me a business card.

"Officer Riley, I believe you. Logic tells me you should go to the police, but my instinct, like yours, says to wait. I, like the rest of the board and senior staff at Illcom, have been fully interrogated by the police. I'm pretty sure I'm not a suspect, so I think it's safe to call me if you need help. In exchange, I expect you to tell me whatever you find out."

"I can do that."

"Good, because my business is at stake, and so is my life. And yours. I don't think we can wait for the police to sort this all out."

We stood there staring at each other, both surprised to find ourselves in these roles.

"You should leave first," Aldo said, motioning toward the door. "I'll follow in a few minutes."

13

I left Aldo and took a bus to my apartment building. I slid the key into my apartment door and let myself in. It had been two weeks since I'd last been inside, and the entry hall felt oddly alien. The air was stale and the quiet seemed otherworldly. As I moved into the kitchen, the feeling continued. I had changed into dark clothes. With a black knit cap covering my bright hair, I felt like a thief in my own home. Nothing seemed quite right, and I realized it was more than likely that my apartment had been thoroughly searched by at least the Chicago police and perhaps other interested parties as well. It gave me a shiver as I passed through the living room and into the bedroom, noticing small items that didn't seem to be quite where I had left them.

So far, I had played it pretty smart, if I do say so myself. My investigation hadn't produced any strong leads, but I now had a much better idea of what was going on and whom I was dealing with. Really, it's whom. Unfortunately, my days of smart were over, because going to my apartment was both stupid and dangerous, as I was about to find out.

My gun safe seemed, well, safe. And untampered with. I opened it and sighed with relief at the sight of my Beretta M. I grabbed it and loaded it, took a box of rounds and put them in my satchel. My Glock was still in an evidence locker somewhere at police headquarters. I would not be going there any time soon.

I went to my closet and took my dressy clothes out of my satchel. In their place I shoved my backup uniform, my bathing suit, and some socks and underwear. Somewhere in the bottom of my closet was a pair of old sneakers that I wanted for working out, but I'd be damned if I could find them. I had just gotten down on my knees when I heard the front door click open.

Without thinking, I rolled forward into the closet, pulling the satchel with me, and covering myself with dirty clothes that were heaped on the floor. Fortunately, I had not turned on any lights. There was nothing to give away my presence in the apartment, and the shadows of the dark closet were deep. I crouched in stillness, controlling my breath while slowly slipping my hand into my bag to retrieve my pistol.

Footsteps from hard shoes echoed through the kitchen. There were no voices, but I heard the unintelligible static of a police radio. A sound I knew well.

I remained motionless as the officer moved into the bedroom, though something was poking uncomfortably into my rear end. I held the Beretta tightly in my hand, willing the man or woman to move along.

The radio squawked again, and a woman's voice responded from just a few feet away, near the foot of the bed.

"Copy. There's nothing here... The door was unlocked, so I think she likely came and went... I don't know, maybe she needed her toothbrush... Okay, I'll tell him and come right down."

Whew. I heard her footsteps cross the kitchen and then I heard my front door shut. I exhaled and extricated myself from the dirty clothes. The thing that had been sticking into my butt was one of my missing sneakers. I found the other one and put them both in the satchel, slung it over one shoulder, my gun still in my hand, and left the bedroom.

I crossed the carpeted living room and entered the kitchen, where a male police officer was sitting at my kitchen table, idly thumbing through information on his phone.

Chicago Blue

I gasped out loud, and his head jerked up from the screen, his jaw dropping in surprise.

"Riley!" he shouted, and started to rise, but I had already brought my hand up, pointing my gun directly at his chest.

"Freeze!" I shouted at him, and he did.

He was no one I recognized, but the force has about 12,000 officers, and my apartment wasn't in my precinct, so that was unsurprising. He wasn't that tall, but from his chest and arms I could tell he was someone who frequented the gym. It was common for a lot of the guys to spend an hour before or after shift working out. They start doing it to balance out all the bad food we eat on duty, then it becomes a habit and a vanity.

He started to lower his hands below the table, but I gave him a look that told him I knew that move, and he instead put both hands palm down on the table top, where I could see them. I nodded my approval.

"Riley, you—"

"Stop. Just, shush a minute. I need to think."

"That's obvious."

"What's that supposed to mean?"

"It's just that I told McKinnon there was no way you would come back here, but he insisted on check-ins every four hours. I guess you are dumber than the average terrorist."

Everyone's a critic.

"Listen, jerkwater. I'm not a terrorist—"

He gave a sarcastic snort, which I ignored. I began backing away from him toward the door.

"I'm just a cop like you and I'm going to walk out of here right now and skip past the whole 'Give yourself up' conversation to the part where you had no choice but to let me go."

Chicago Blue

My backward walking skills evidently needed some work, because instead of the hallway to the door, I backed into the little table that holds my sunglasses, phone charger, and a bowl of loose change.

He seized the moment and jumped to his feet, flipping the kitchen table up and at me. My gun discharged accidentally, splintering the table top as I jumped back out of the way. He leapt at me over the upended table, but his foot caught on its edge and fell heavily unto his hands and knees. I took a strong forward step and snap-kicked him in his face as hard as I could. He howled and instinctively grabbed his nose with one hand. I swept his supporting arm and he fell unto his shoulder, rolling onto his back. I moved four or five steps back and kept the Beretta trained on him.

We both flinched as his radio burst into life, a frantic voice shouting. The gunshot would have officers here in seconds. His partner probably wasn't even to the ground floor yet. I had to get out of there, but for some reason I was too furious to move.

"What the hell is *wrong* with you!?" I shouted at him. I was holding my gun with both hands now, and they were shaking hard, the barrel bobbing around but still pointed firmly at him. He held his nose with both hands, blood flowing out around them. "I could have *killed* you!" I continued, in a rage now. "Are you freaking *crazy*?!"

He just moaned, and then the radio burst to life again, breaking me from my trance, and I turned and ran from the apartment. I rushed down the hallway and past the stairwell, heading for the other stairwell at the far end, assuming there wouldn't be enough police on hand yet to secure the entire building. As I ran, I tucked the pistol into the back of my black jeans, below the bottom of the my bag, which was bouncing against my back as I ran.

Chicago Blue

I sprinted down four of the five floors and then burst through the door and down another long hall. I skidded to a stop in front of 204, and pulled my keys from my pocket, fumbling until I found Mrs. Lowicki's. When she went to Arizona to visit her sister, Mrs. Gagnon from next door would walk her dog and water her plants, but she always left me a key as well, just in case. I eased the door shut quietly behind me and turned to find Gizmo, her crazy three-legged dog, staring up at me. I bent down and gave him a quick pat, and then moved quickly to the back bedroom of the apartment. The dog followed me, curious, but he didn't bark. The windows here overlooked the alley behind the apartment building, and I opened the window and the screen and tossed my bag out. I lowered myself until the drop was only about ten feet and let go, cushioning my landing with my knees and managing not to break my ankle.

The alley was deserted, and as I ran I could hear my own voice pounding in my head with each step: "Stupid! Stupid! Stupid! Stupid!"

14

We ate Chinese food glumly, watching the evening news. I was all over it. Fugitive cop, assaulting a police officer. Now believed to still be in the city. My photo. They had managed to find a decent picture of me from a squad softball game we did for charity a few years ago. Apparently they had decided that it was bad for optics to keep showing my police portrait, in which I am clearly wearing a Chicago Police uniform. I turned down the sound after they repeated the same information for the fourth time.

"What," said Ruby in a slow, disgusted voice, "could you possibly have been thinking?"

"Needed my bathing suit," I said in a dull voice, my mouth full of lo mein.

"Honestly, you spent three thousand dollars on designer clothes, but you couldn't buy a bathing suit?"

"You know how hard it is to get one that fits right!? Once you find the right one, you hold on to it."

"I've got a question," interjected Marty, who was still watching the news.

"Nike. Red," I answered. "I'm hoping for a sponsorship or for product placement when they make a movie about this."

"That wasn't my question," he said. He got up to bring his plate to the sink, stopping to grimace at the milk stain I had left on his friend's carpet. I don't know what he was upset about. I was pretty sure I'd be able to get that out. "If our villain is from some outside company, how are we ever going to find them?"

"I know. This would be so much easier if it were Farnham, or Valerie Archer. There could be a dozen different tech companies wanting to horn in on their business, and we are talking billions of dollars. With a 'B' billions. I'm sure there are plenty of people willing to commit a few murders to get a bigger piece of that."

"Not only that," added Marty, "but it doesn't even have to be a telecommunications company. There is so much consolidation now, it could be a hardware company, or a cloud storage company, or a big bank for that matter, wanting an opportunity to enter the field."

"Great," said Ruby. "I feel so much better now. Optimistic. I think we need to focus on getting you out of the city, out of the country even."

"But I need to figure this out."

"Do you? Look at me," Ruby said in a stern voice. "I was interrogated twice last week. They know we are friends."

I gasped. Of course they did, that made perfect sense. Marty looked concerned.

"What if they are following you, Auntie?"

"They're not," said Ruby calmly. "I made sure."

"You made sure?"

"Trust me, Martin. I know how to lose a tail," she said in such a deadpan voice that I burst out laughing.

"I do," she said, looking hurt. "But, my point is, you are their best lead, and you have no lead. Eventually, they will find you. Or worse, the killers will find you!"

I sighed and looked at myself, once again being featured on the television.

"This would have killed my dad," I said morosely.

"I'm sure he'd be very proud of you, Red," said Marty.

"Don't call me Red."

"He was a police officer?"

"Yeah. For thirty years. From a family of criminals. His brother Patrick spent a lot of time in jail. His brother Nicholas was a high-powered businessman, in various businesses, none of which my father approved of."

Chicago Blue

"He must have been happy you became a cop!" said Marty brightly.

"He died before that," I said. "He would *not* have been happy. He wanted more than anything for me to become a lawyer. That was his gift to me when I started college," I added, pointing to the leather bag on the floor in the corner. "But after his heart attack, and with Mom already at Highland Acres, I don't know. I couldn't do the school work. My heart wasn't in it."

"I'm sorry, honey," said Ruby.

I sprang off the couch and sang, in my best Sinatra voice: "Regrets! I've had a few..."

They both stared at me.

"Just trying to lighten the mood," I grinned and looked again at the silent talking heads on the news. "They have no idea where I am," I said, distractedly.

"Thank goodness for that," said Ruby. Then she saw the look on my face. "What is it?"

"I have another tremendously bad idea..."

15

There was a fight about the gun. First there was a fight about the plan, which I admit was full of holes and left too much to chance. Then, there was a fight about the gun. I refused to bring my Beretta. Ruby went ballistic.

"Are you out of your mind?"

"This is nonnegotiable, Ruby."

"These people are not fucking around, pardon my Czech," Ruby spat in a quiet voice. The cupcake shop we were sitting in was mostly empty, but still, language.

"Have you ever fired your gun in the line of duty?" I asked.

"No," she admitted.

"I almost killed a cop," I whispered. "First by accident, then on purpose. If he came at me again, I would have shot him in the chest."

"They are trying to kill you," she said evenly.

"He wasn't. He was just a cop, like us."

"Yes, but in this case, you've invited everyone to the party, haven't you? If your plan works, those men in black are going to be here, and they want you dead."

"I know," I grimaced, and almost lost my appetite for the vanilla strawberry cupcake sitting in front of me. Almost. "But that's why I want the police there as well. They won't go shooting everybody if the cops are there. Not me, not any other innocent bystanders."

Ruby shook her head. "This is going to be a giant cluster."

"Thanks for the vote of confidence," I smirked.

She stood up. "You know it's just because I can't be there that I'm so upset."

"You can't, you—"

"I know, I know. Plus, I run way too slowly," she said, shaking her cane.

Chicago Blue

"We've got to go, the place will be empty by now." I shoved a last piece of cupcake in my mouth and we headed out the door.

So, my batshit crazy plan. I didn't know who the bad guys were, or where they were. They could be anyone. They knew who I was, but they didn't know where I was. And, most importantly, they didn't know what I looked like now. So, all I had to do was let them know where and when I was going to be in public, and then be hiding when they showed up. Identify them, follow them, get whatever information we could get. Easy, right?

Ruby wasn't so sure. One minute she was convinced they wouldn't take the bait. Next minute she was convinced there would be a hundred of them, they'd recognize me right away, and I'd be slaughtered. Her reasons for it being a bad idea kept changing, but her underlying unease remained.

That's where the cops came in. I assumed our mystery men were no friend of the police, so we would make sure they showed up as well.

We chose a chic little hair salon on East Walton, not far from where I'd had my recent adventure at The Drake. It was a busy street on a Friday afternoon, and that would hopefully work in our favor. I walked to the salon and entered. Two women were cleaning up their workstations. I set down my bag on the counter and said, "Hi. I'm Katrin, from Lakeshore Media."

They greeted me, and showed me around the place. I took a light meter out of my bag and held it up every now and then.

"I love your hair," said one of them, whose hair was also a bright red. "Who does it?"

"Martin," I replied simply. Then I conspicuously looked at the clock on the wall.

Chicago Blue

"Oh," said the other one, who was taller and quite a bit older than the redhead. "Are you sure we can't stay and watch? It's so exciting!"

"I'm afraid not. Mr. Arnesto is quite particular, but you have my assurance, nothing will be damaged. We won't even move anything, he wants it just as it is."

She swelled with pride. "OK then, we'll be back in two hours," she said, picking up her hand bag.

"Great," I said with a cheerful smile. "When you come back we can talk about getting you a set of the finished shoot. For your own promotional use."

I closed the door behind them. Out of my bag I took a sign that said, "Appointment Only," and hung it on the door. I didn't want any innocent bystanders, just in case things went wild.

I walked over to one of the hairdresser's stations and caught myself in the mirror. My vivid red hair had a bit of gel in it, and the sides were freshly shaved. With Ruby's help I had removed my stiches, and the flop of hair concealed the scar. I wore black cat glasses and I had dangly earrings in each ear, about six jangly bracelets on each wrist, and a clip-on nose ring. I was wearing my leather pants (finally!!) and a white tank top that showed the fake dragon tattoo I had applied on the back of my shoulder. I know, right? I turned to see how the leather pants looked from behind. They looked great.

My Doc Martens sounded loud on the floor as I crossed back to the front door to keep a lookout for big black SUVs.

The day after formulating my plan, Marty used a fake online persona to hire a photographer named Gil Arnesto to do a fashion shoot at the Zaza Salon. It had to be that salon, because the editor he worked for had come across it one day and *simply* loved it. (This next bit, in the movie

Chicago Blue

of my life, will be an excellent montage. I'm hoping Bruno Mars will do the music.)

Ruby picked up a new cell phone for me in Evanston, programmed with my old number. It seemed certain that they had used my phone to follow me when they first hunted me down on Lake Shore Drive and tried to kill me. Ruby thought it was unlikely they would still be monitoring that number, but Marty thought certain that they would be. I turned the phone on and called the Zaza Salon, making an appointment for Friday afternoon. "Could I please have my long hair dyed bright blue?" Sure I could. As soon as the call was over, I pulled the card from the phone and hopped on the "L" and got out of that part of town. Half an hour later, I got off the train, leaving the SIM card behind, and looked for a payphone. I gotta say, payphones seem to be a thing of the past. I could only think of one, and it was a dozen blocks away in an Osco. I finally found one in a hotel lobby and called the Zaza to cancel my appointment.

Marty had converted some Bitcoin into a certified check that was used as a down payment for Arnesto. I delivered it in the guise of an intern for *Fashion Couture* magazine. Arnesto contacted the salon and made arrangements to use the space, uninterrupted, for two hours on Friday afternoon. It would be great publicity for the salon. Later that day Marty called Arnesto and canceled the shoot, letting him keep the down payment. He told Arnesto that he had already told the owner of the salon that the shoot was canceled, but of course he had done no such thing. As a result, I now had the place all to myself.

I opened the front door just slightly so that I could get an angle that let me look all the way down to Michigan Ave. I turned and looked the other way to make sure Marty was in place, on the sidewalk just across from the cupcake place, tourist camera at the ready. He appeared to be taking pictures of pigeons on the rooftops.

I turned back the other direction just in time to see a black SUV with tinted windows racing up the street toward me. I broke out in a cold sweat, ducking back into the shop and rushing to the phone on the back counter.

"911, what's your emergency?"

"I'm at the hairdressers on Walton," I whispered hurriedly. "There's a woman having her hair dyed blue. I'm sure it's the woman from the news, with the bombs."

"Is she—" I slammed the phone down and stepped to the nearest workstation as the SUV pulled up directly across the street and parked illegally. Man, these guys were jerks, I thought. They didn't even put their flashers on.

Three men in dark suits and sunglasses sprung from the vehicle. They were all about the same size, and had the exact same short haircut, but while two of them had dark hair, one of them was a blond. They crossed the street toward me. I snatched up a can of hairspray in one hand and a glass container filled with combs in a blue liquid in the other, turning toward the mirror as they burst through the door.

"Freeze!" the blond yelled, pulling a gun. Guess they were going full bad cop.

I screamed and dropped the glass jar, which shattered on the floor spraying blue disinfectant everywhere. The blond one reached me and shoved me back against the workstation, gun in my face, while the other two rushed into the back room, having drawn pistols of their own.

I screamed again, and Blondie leaned harder against me, grabbing my neck with one hand and pressing the gun under my chin with the other. "Shut up!" he screamed into my face.

Chicago Blue

The other two returned from the back room.

"Clear," they both said at once.

"Where is she?" Blondie spat at me.

I just blubbered.

"Tell me!"

"Who?" I spluttered, "who?"

"You had an appointment at 3PM. Where is she?"

"She was early," I gasped, gulping. "I finished dyeing her hair and she left about 10 minutes ago."

He half threw me across the room to the counter near the front door.

"I want her information," he rasped. "From the appointment."

I put my left hand on the strap of my leather bag, which was sitting on the counter.

"Are you the police?" I demanded in a shaky voice.

"Yeah, we're the police," snarled one of the other two with a sneer.

"You can't treat me like this. I'll call the mayor!"

Blondie started toward me when we heard the sound of approaching police sirens. They all froze for a second, during which I snatched my bag off the counter and pushed quickly out the door. The window next to me shattered at the same instant I heard a gun fire. I dropped to the sidewalk and scooted between two cars stopped in traffic, dragging my bag behind me. I popped up on the other side and chanced a look back across the hood of a silver Jaguar. Through the smashed window of the salon I saw them start toward me, but as the sirens wailed more loudly they stopped, turned, and headed to the back.

Across the street the SUV roared to life and careened out into traffic. They must have left a driver in the vehicle. I watched it screech around the corner, then suddenly realized I was standing in the middle of traffic with police cars less than a block away. I had to get out of there!

As I turned to run the Jaguar beeped its horn. It was such a polite, friendly "beep beep" that I turned to look at the driver, who had rolled down her window.

There, wearing a fashionable pair of sunglasses, was the unmistakable face of the woman from Farnham's office. White catsuit woman!

"Need a lift?" she asked, with a mischievous grin.

I turned and ran across the street and through the first door I came to. I rushed through racks of snowboards and winter clothes and out the rear fire door, setting off an alarm. I raced down the alley opposite, and then ducked behind a parked car. I pulled a long black wig and an orange button-down sweater from my bag and put them on.

Two minutes later I was sitting at the bar at Ditka's Restaurant, wondering what drink went best with adrenaline and fear.

16

I kept my head down self-consciously as my hard shoes slapped the linoleum floor of the hospital hallway. It felt strange to be back in uniform. These were my own clothes, but I felt more an imposter than in any of the disguises I had worn so far. I kept my hat down low over my face and held a bouquet of flowers in front of me, blocking where my name tag would usually be pinned.

The intensive care unit was quiet. There didn't seem to be much police presence on hand, except for me. Just one officer near the nurse's station, and he was easy enough to sneak around—he was busy chatting up one of the nurses. They must have decided that Vincente wasn't in any further danger, though I'm not sure what they based that on. If someone was trying to remove the leadership of Illcom, they had failed with Arthur Vincente and Aldo Frances. They were both still alive.

I entered his room quietly to find a woman seated next to the bed. Her hands were folded and her head was resting on her chest. She was either praying or asleep, I wasn't sure which. She was plump, but expensively dressed. Her hair was curly and had likely been colored, as it was a dark brown, even though she must have been close to seventy years old.

I was hesitating in the doorway, not wanting to disturb her, when she suddenly gave a jerk of her head and opened her eyes, pulling herself up straight.

"Oh," she said, in a lovely voice, "hello there."

I stepped into the room and placed the flowers on a side table below the television, which hung from the ceiling. I sat quickly on the other chair in the room.

"Hi," I said with a smile. "I'm Riley Wilcox, from the citizen relations office of the Chicago Police."

Chicago Blue

"There was a young man on duty here, a moment ago," she said with a puzzled look around. "I'm not sure where he's gone."

"Don't worry, he's just down the hall. I just spoke with him a moment ago. I'm just here to see how you are doing, Mrs. Vincente. To see if there's anything we could do for you."

Her face lost its smile. "Well, you could find out who did this to my Arthur."

"I'm so sorry," I said, trying hard not to scratch my itchy blond wig. "So, Mr. Vincente hasn't said anything at all yet?"

She looked at me strangely.

"I'm afraid you haven't heard, Miss. Wilcox. Arthur hasn't woken up, and he's not expected to ever wake up." Her voice broke at the end and she began to sob, leaving me feeling like a jerk.

"I'm so sorry, I didn't realize. I was only just assigned this case."

"Yes, well," said Mrs. Vincente, who really seemed like a class act. "It's okay, dear. I really don't care anymore if they find out who did this. You'd think it would be the top thing on my mind, but what's the point?"

"Well, for one thing, ma'am, we need to make sure that you yourself aren't in any danger."

"Me? Why on earth me?"

I sat on the edge of my chair and straightened my back.

"It's possible, ma'am, that this was done by someone close to Mr. Vincente, and therefore close to you as well."

She looked aghast.

"Surely this is about Illcom, and the other explosion, the one at the Farnham Building."

"Yes, that is likely. But that doesn't mean that someone from one of those two companies wasn't the perpetrator. Can you think of anyone who was particularly upset, or angry, at Mr. Vincente or Mr. Blalock over the last few months?"

She looked up and to her right, absentmindedly searching her memory.

"Arthur was the Chair of the Board. So of course there could be someone else on the board who was jealous of him, but I'm afraid I just don't know. I think his appointment as interim CEO was unanimous. It doesn't really make any sense at all." She began to cry again. "He spent so much time helping that company, though I'm not sure why."

"Did he work for Illcom before joining the board?"

She pulled a tissue from her sleeve, just like my grandmother always used to do, and wiped her nose.

"No, just as a consultant. Arthur worked for Ma Bell way, way back. Then when they broke up, he headed up sales and marketing for AT&T in the early days. Lord, he could've convinced Alexander Graham Bell himself that he needed another phone line in his house."

I laughed, even though she'd probably told that joke ten thousand times, and nodded encouragingly.

"Ferris Farnham hired him as a consultant when they rolled out their first subscriber plans—back then people weren't quite sure how to handle the voice and the data, both on the same phone. It was all new."

"Mmhmm," I agreed.

"Well, he did such a good job that Carter Blalock hired him too." She looked over at her husband's motionless form. "Over the years I think he came to like Carter the better of the two. Ferris Farnham can be a bit of a cold fish." She made a face. "A bit holier than thou, if you know what I mean."

I leaned forward.

Chicago Blue

"Do you think Mr. Farnham could have had something to do with it?"

She shook her head.

"It doesn't seem like he would have it in him, but then who? That's just what I keep asking myself. Who? Who would want to do this? It doesn't make any sense."

"We will find out," I assured her as I rose to my feet. My time was running out.

"You know what?" she said, standing also. "Good! I know I said it doesn't matter, but I've changed my mind. I *do* care who did this. It's not right. He was a good man, a good black man who grew up in a rough part of this city and made himself rich and successful." She was building up a head of steam now, and I began to back toward the door.

"If the police don't find out who did this," she continued. "I will. I've got the energy, the money, and all the time in the world, now that Arthur is gone. They better watch out!"

"Yes, ma'am. Yes, indeed," I agreed, and took my leave.

17

Belinda Blalock seemed surprised to find someone at her front gate who wasn't a reporter. At least the woman said she wasn't a reporter; more than one journalist had given false credentials to try to get an interview.

She looked again at the security monitor. The woman drove a fairly nice Lexus; it didn't look like the kind of car a journalist would drive. Ditto the very fashionable suit. She hit the buzzer, and the heavy metal gate rolled slowly to the side.

A few minutes later, Mrs. Blalock perused the business card she was handed. "Wilcox Reinsurance?" she asked. "I don't think I've heard of it."

"Well," said the woman, who had introduced herself as Hadley Neff, "reinsurance companies insure insurance companies. I know that sounds ridiculous, but—"

"I know what reinsurance is," said Blalock in a pointed voice.

"You do?" chirped Neff brightly. "Fantastic! You have no idea how much time I spend explaining it to people. People you really think should already understand such things," she added in a conspiratorial undertone. She had bobbed blond hair, a lightly freckled nose under fairly thick glasses, and a nervous habit of crossing and recrossing her legs as she sat.

"What's this all about, Mrs. Neff?" asked Blalock. "I have an incredibly busy schedule, as you can imagine, and most of the insurance issues are covered by Illcom people..."

"Call me Hadley, please," said Hadley Neff. "And no Mrs., I'm afraid," she chuckled, mostly to herself. "Just me, and the cats. Jay-Z and Beyonce. And Mittens. And Fluffers, of course."

Belinda Blalock cleared her throat.

Chicago Blue

"Yes, sorry. I know you've suffered a terrible, terrible loss, and I wouldn't presume to trouble you at home, it's just that…"

Neff crossed her legs uncomfortably and adjusted her glasses, looking uncomfortable.

"Yes?"

"Well, when I was going through everything on our end I noticed that none of the considerable coverage listed you as a beneficiary, or your daughter. I just wanted to make sure that there wasn't something, ah, 'unusual' going on."

Blalock raised her eyebrows. "Unusual? Yes, I see what you mean, and I thank you for your diligence, but Gracie and I have nothing to do with Illcom at all."

"You don't?"

"No, we never have. There are completely separate trusts for the two of us, funded by Carter's early successes. We don't own any part of Illcom."

"Well," said Neff, with a sigh of relief, "that is wonderful to hear! Just wonderful! I'm embarrassed, however, that I wasn't properly briefed. I am going to have a stern word with Jerry K. when I get back to the office. We call him Jerry K. because there's another Jerry, Jerry Bingham. We call him Jerry—"

"B, yes, I see. You'll forgive my impatience," Blalock said, rising and smoothing her cream skirt, "but is there anything else I can do for you, Ms. Neff?"

Hadley stood. "Well no, that should do it! Just, I guess I'm a bit confused. If not you and Gracie, then who takes ownership of all of Mr. Blalock's shares of Illcom?"

"Well, the same as always, you know, there's always been an agreement that…"

"Yes?"

Chicago Blue

"Well," mused Belinda Blalock, her eyes narrowing, "it seems to me that you should either already know that, or perhaps you aren't supposed to know that at all."

"Yes, ha ha, I see what you mean!" the woman laughed, reaching up to adjust her glasses again. Only this time one of her rings caught in her hair, and when she dropped her hand back down she inadvertently pulled the blonde wig from her head, revealing a bright red swoop of hair.

Blalock jumped back.

"What the hell?"

That's right, it was me, if you hadn't guessed, and I had just earned myself a photo in the spy's encyclopedia under the listing for "Blown Cover."

I tried to shake the wig off my hand, but it was really stuck on the ring. Still shaking my hand, I started to back toward the front door, but Belinda leapt forward and grabbed my wrist, hard. Tennis player, I'm guessing.

"I know who you are!" Her excitement made her bold, and frankly stupid, if I were really a dangerous criminal. I stepped toward her rather than away, throwing her off balance, and struck her in the solar plexus with my right fist. Oh Jesus, now I was assaulting widows. Just add it to the list.

She might be in great shape, but she was not used to being hit, and I took the moment of her surprise and shock to yank my left hand out of her grip. I turned and raced to the door, not looking back until I had reached it and yanked it open.

She was kneeling on one knee on the carpet, one hand on the arm of the sofa and the other clutching her chest. I stood still for several seconds until she finally got her wind back with a huge, rattling gasp.

"I'm so sorry!" I blurted, then turned and ran from the house. The woman was having the worst month of her

Chicago Blue

life, and I had just added a strange, unprovoked assault to the list of things no one should ever have to endure.

Outside, I made for the stolen Lexus, but halfway there I noticed that the driveway gate was closed—I was not getting out by car. I tracked right and hit the fence with a running jump, just able to use my momentum to grab the top and haul myself up and over the seven-foot railing.

On the way over and down my skirt caught on the spikes, and with a horrible, expensive ripping sound I flopped to the ground, landing on my ass and my elbows. I looked up at where my skirt still hung from the top of the fence, swore, and then turned my head to find myself looking directly into the security camera, mounted on the top of the gatehouse wall.

"Crap," I said aloud. I was going to be on the six o'clock news, again, for sure. This time with my underpants showing, and not my most stylish pair. I struggled to my feet, put the wig back on my head, and looked around quickly. Response time out here was probably about ten minutes, unless there happened to be a cruiser already in the area. I'd better get going and get out of sight.

The skirt was still hanging from the top of the fence, and was clearly a lost cause. I took off my suit jacket and wrapped it around my waist, holding it closed with one hand as I trotted past several leafy Glencoe estates, behind the Center for Jewish Living, and into the kitchen entrance of the Lake Shore Country Club, where I called Ruby to come and get me while I hid in the bathroom. The world's most glamorous spy.

The look on Ruby's face held an entire lecture. I slumped into the passenger's seat and averted my eyes.

We drove in silence for all of two minutes.

"I'm sorry," I began, but she cut me off.

Chicago Blue

"That woman and her child were kidnapped. *Kidnapped*!"

I looked over at her in surprise. "What are you talking about?"

"I just got my hand on the report," Ruby elaborated. "Three men, one blond and two dark-haired, in dark suits—"

"That sounds familiar," I snorted.

"You bet your *zadku*. Unfortunately, they look so nondescript that the description doesn't help. Took them from their car outside the Art Institute. She was chaperoning her daughter's school trip."

Oh boy, here it comes. I slouched down in my seat like a teenager.

"Because she's a *good person*, Kay. And they took her and her daughter and held them until Carter Blalock put a bomb on his arm and walked into the Farnham Building."

"Oh, my god."

"And you broke into her house! And you stole a goddamn car."

"It's just that—"

"No. Quiet. I'm helping you. I'll keep helping you." She turned a corner aggressively, her anger coming out in her driving. "But you've got to slow down and be thinking this through. You want to become a criminal?"

"No. Maybe. I don't know."

"Maybe?"

I turned in my seat to look at her. "Ruby. This whole thing has been crazy. But it's made me realize how unhappy I was."

"And becoming a criminal will make you happy?"

"It's not that. It's just that, for the first time—and in a really intense way—I feel free. And alive."

She shook her head and sighed.

Chicago Blue

"Well, you'll be neither of those things if the police or the men in black catch up with you. You need to lay low for a while."

"I promise."

"Are you hungry?"

"Starving."

18

I laid low for the next four weeks. Too many close calls, one after the other. Plus, I was waiting on some information. Among other things, Marty was researching the other Illcom board members to see if there were any possible leads there. He wanted to take a look at their individual financial situations, to see if any of them had made large investments that were in any way connected to the success or failure of Farnham or Illcom. Obviously, what he was doing was highly illegal, which I have to say didn't bother me nearly as much as I thought it would. It was just taking a really long time.

Ruby, too, was putting in some time researching, only in her case it was police files. Getting access to this information also took a long time, because Ruby had to make absolutely certain no one was watching her. Obviously, the fact that we had been friends put her in the hot seat. She had to play it safe.

I had, indeed, been on the six o'clock news that night. Kathy Brock was chatting with an expert about why I would still be in the Chicago area, while a still photo of me sprawled on Belinda Blalock's driveway was inserted in the upper corner of the screen. Mercifully, they had cropped the picture from chest to head, so you couldn't see my white granny panties. I was going to have to get some underwear that matched the sophistication of my new wardrobe.

Mrs. Vincente was also on the news, berating the police for not being able to catch me, even though I was publicly flaunting myself all over town.

I hung around the campus and mostly worked out, a combination of swimming, indoor cycling, and weight training. I missed my old yoga class, and tried to do some on my own, but it just wasn't the same. I give up

Chicago Blue

too easily when I'm on my own. All my injuries from the explosion had healed, and I was feeling good, stronger than ever. My headaches were gone, I was off the meds, and even though my hair was short, you could only barely see the scar.

I kept my hair short because it made the wig thing easier, and I was wearing a wig all the time now, even to work out, ever since my bright red punk look had been broadcast on the nightly news. Sweating in a wig really sucks.

That disastrous night, after Ruby had picked me up and we had managed to make it back to my safe house (that's what I'm calling it), I shaved my head all the way, down to about three quarters of an inch. The magenta was gone, and I just had a buzz cut of my own red hair, slowly growing back out.

Kathy Brock's question was a good one: Why was I still in the city? I hoped the Chicago Police were also considering this question. Why was I still around? Maybe, just maybe, it would keep them digging deeper into the case, and if they did they would find some new leads. On the other hand, it might just make them look even harder for me. I was kinda making them look like chumps by popping up every few days and then escaping. I think the most recent footage made it clear to John Q. Public that I was not a criminal mastermind.

Part of the answer was, of course, that I wanted to clear my name. Another part of the answer was the problem of my identity. I needed a fake license and a fake passport. Not just in case I needed to get out of the city, but also for continuing the investigation. Renting a car as Hadley Neff would have been a lot safer than stealing one. That was just one example.

I had a pretty good idea how to go about getting the fakes I needed, but I was going to have to go see my

Chicago Blue

mom for that, and I was a little worried that she might be under surveillance, even though it was highly unlikely there was any help she could offer the police.

My musing was interrupted when my phone—which had been pumping some old school No Doubt into my ears while I cycled in the gym—cut the music to tell me I had a call from Marty. Finally, I thought. Laying low was getting a little boring, although my calves were really starting to look great.

We met at my place on campus, because Ruby deemed it safer if I didn't travel around, unless it was necessary. She had picked up some ćevapčići and rice from Restaurant Sarajevo and Marty had brought some beer.

I figured I'd burned enough calories to earn a beer, so I helped myself. Plus, I wasn't really trying to lose weight as much as put on muscle and get more flexible. So there.

Marty made me wait until we had finished eating before he opened his bag and pulled out some papers.

"Nada on the rest of the Illcom board," he said, apologetically. "They are all pretty clean. As clean as industry tycoons can be, I guess."

I pulled the papers toward me and whistled at the top one. This is what I had been waiting for, the results of our downtown caper at the hair salon.

Exhibit A was a close-up of the woman in the Jaguar. She had completely freaked me out with the way she honked and waved to me, for a couple of reasons. One, I was pretty sure she hadn't seen me in Farnham's office. And if that was the case, why did she give me that funny grin? I was certain she was toying with me, in a "I know who you really are" kind of way. Which meant she was better at seeing through disguises than the others.

Chicago Blue

Two, it was no accident that she had shown up at that showdown. That meant she was somehow connected to my case. Up until this point, I had left open the idea that she was in Farnham's office coincidentally, pulling off some corporate espionage that had nothing to do with me. That seemed less plausible now.

And C, she hadn't gotten out of the car and chased me. In fact, she seemed fairly amused by the whole thing. This freaked me out more than anything, because how do I deal with this woman when I have no idea what her motives are? She seemed unconcerned that I was getting away. Hopefully ID-ing her would shed some light.

"No luck," said Marty, reading my thoughts. "Unless her name is Wilhelmina Schmidt and she lives in Sauganash."

"She doesn't much look like a Wilhelmina," said Ruby.

"Or a Schmidt for that matter," replied Marty, "though I wouldn't mind getting a closer look."

I rolled my eyes.

"I don't think she's big into video games, Marty, I'm sorry to say."

"Hey!" he said, undeterred. "I have plenty of other interests besides video games."

"Stolen car?" I asked, though I knew the answer.

"Stolen car," he confirmed. "Sorry."

"It's alright," I said. "Old Wilhelmina drives a pretty awesome Jag." I gave a little Balkan salad burp. "Excuse me! Anyway, I wish we knew who she was, because she's freaking me out." I decided to move on. "How about the moron triplets?"

"Quadruplets," interjected Ruby. "Don't forget the one driving the car."

"Yes," Marty said enthusiastically, pulling pictures of the SUV out of the stack. "Much better luck here. I don't know the names of any of the goons, but the vehicle is registered to Fitzgerald Security, right downtown."

"Security?" asked Ruby. "They seemed more like hired thugs."

"Well, you can't really call yourself Fitzgerald Hired Thugs, Ruby. I suppose a security company is as good a cover as any."

"It's better than a cover," said Marty. "It's a real business deal. They may do some shady things on the side, but they make a boatload of money as a serious security firm. They've got some big-time clients." He grinned expectantly at me. "Anyone? Anyone? Bueller?"

"Okay, I'll bite. Who?"

He grimaced. "But that was the hint—Anyone? Beuller?"

"Ferris Farnham!"

"I'm missing something," Ruby complained, looking back and forth between us.

"It's a movie, Ruby," I explained. "*Ferris Beuller's Day Off*."

"Seriously Auntie? You've lived in Chicago for 40 years and you don't know *Ferris Bueller's Day Off*?"

"I prefer the classics."

"But it *is* a classic, Auntie! One of the greats!"

"Okay," I interrupted. "Moving on to things that matter. Is that it on Fitzgerald?"

"No," said Marty. "It gets better. They sometimes pay a consultant, an expert who used to work for them about 20 years ago named..."

"Bueller?" asked Ruby.

"No," replied Marty. "Not Beuller. His name is Greg Ralston."

19

"Can you sit still for two minutes?"

It was one of those days when you realize what you really need are a few new henchmen. Don't get me wrong, Marty was great. Hacking into the DMV was movie-star-level awesome. The kid has a future as a cyber criminal. However, he fidgets like crazy, and three hours in a car doing nothing but watching Fitzgerald Security's front entrance felt like a lifetime.

Ruby wasn't much better. Her leg would start to cramp after an hour or so, and she would have to get out and stretch and take a walk. This meant we had to park even further away so that no one would notice her getting out of the car every 45 minutes, walking up and down the sidewalk, and then getting back in the car. Oh, and twice, she fell asleep. Sometimes I swear she is eighty years old.

This was day two of the great surveillance, and I have to say it's maybe a good thing I never made detective when I was on the force. I liked walking a beat. Even patrolling in the cruiser, you didn't get much exercise, but at least the scenery kept changing. But this, this was mind-numbing.

I was eating yet another salad, trying to offset all the sedentary hours. Marty was eating a bag of Doritos. Yet another bag of Doritos. I'm glad it was his car, because the interior by this time was covered with orange cheese powder. It looked like the surface of Mars. At least I think it was his car. I was getting better about not asking Marty anything about his work or his skill set. He claimed nothing he did was illegal, but I have to say, from the little I could glean, I'm not sure he had a very good sense of where the legal lines were drawn. On the other hand, I'm sure all those people who work in finance down on

Chicago Blue

LaSalle think they aren't doing anything dubious either. I'm old-fashioned. I like to see actual money, moving from person to bank to person. When everything is happening in nanoseconds in the nanosphere, I feel confused and a bit paranoid.

"Marty," I said, closing my empty salad container. I put it in the plastic bag I was using to collect our stakeout garbage.

"Mmph?" he replied, still chewing a mouthful of chips, binoculars held up to his eyes.

"I'm not sure I've properly thanked you for all the help you've given me. You have literally saved my life."

"Don't mention it," Marty said, without lowering the binoculars.

"If there's anything I can do to pay you back..." I began.

He lowered the binoculars and looked over at me, waggling his eyebrows suggestively.

"Umm, no. That's not happening."

He swallowed his Doritos and laughed. "I'm just kidding. Don't get me wrong, you are a beautiful woman, and I love spending hours in this car with you, which is starting to smell just a little bit like old food, but you are, how should I put it, a bit too mature for me."

I swatted him on the shoulder.

"I'm thirty-three!"

"Eeeexactly," he replied, as if I had just proven his point.

"Seriously," I pressed on. "I don't have a lot of money, but can I—"

"One million dollars!"

"What?"

"I know you are poor now, but when this is all over, you can pay me a million dollars. In Bitcoin."

Chicago Blue

"Martin Martynek, if I make it through this alive, I'll give you a million dollars."

"Deal."

"Heads up, there's Blondie." I motioned toward the building, where our cheerful friend had just exited the front door and headed for a black Ford Taurus, one of six in a row that were likely owned by the company. Either that or these guys all had exactly the same taste.

"Jesus, you're right. How did he get in there without us seeing him?"

"I don't know, we haven't exactly been doing 24-hour surveillance. We didn't get here until about 7 AM. Maybe he was working the night shift and is just getting off."

I looked at my watch; it was just about 1 PM.

"Or," thought Marty aloud, "maybe there's a back door?"

"Just follow," I snapped. "Or would you like me to drive? I'm an excellent driver."

"No, I've got it, Officer Riley. He won't lose me!"

"Okay, but he shouldn't be trying to lose you, because he shouldn't have any idea he is being followed."

It turned out that Marty did just fine as a stalker. He kept back far enough to avoid suspicion, but close enough that we never lost sight of him. In the end, Blondie parked on a nice street in Rogers Park and walked up to a row of townhouse condos. He pulled a set of keys from his pocket and let himself in.

"What now?" asked Marty.

"Nothing now. We go home and I think up a plan. We can't just follow him around all day and hope he meets with the bad guys, and then maybe they accidentally drop a piece of paper on which they've written out their secret plan along with a few Venn diagrams explaining how all this fits together!"

Chicago Blue

"Do you have a gun?" asked Marty, turning to look at me.

"Are you crazy?"

"I can knock on the door, he's never seen me. He unlocks it and you pull the gun on him."

"No."

"We ask him a few questions, he answers as if his life depended on it, we get out of there."

I turned to him as we sat parked on Sheridan.

"Look, I am grateful for all your help, but this is *not* a game. I'm terrified, every time that I ask you or Ruby for help, that something is going to happen to one of you. This guy shot at me in the salon, remember that? He *shot* at me. I don't want to put anyone at risk, but I can't do this alone, either." I banged my fist on the dashboard. "It is soooo frustrating, I want to scream."

"I know it's not a game, but if w—" Marty tried to interject.

"But we don't kill people. End of story. And let me tell you something," I continued, rolling over his objection, "when you pull a gun on someone, you are multiplying exponentially the chance that someone is going to get shot. And then killed."

"But—"

"I'm not going to do it. Alright?!"

I had been leaning across the handbrake and into his face, but now I flopped back into the passenger's seat. I was beginning to cry, and that made me angry.

"I'm sorry," said Marty.

"I know, I know," I said, wiping my eyes with my sleeve. "You just want to help, and I need your help. That much is obvious. But it's got to be on my terms, okay? I take the risks, you and Ruby provide the backup. That doesn't mean you aren't in danger as well. Believe me I realize that. I just want to make sure *you* realize that as well."

"I can take care of myself," Marty said, puffing up slightly.

"Oh Jesus, it's like you didn't hear a word out of my mouth. Let's get out of here."

"We aren't going in?"

"We aren't. I am. And I need to do some prep and I need you to pick up a few things I'm going to need."

It was around 7 PM when I returned with Ruby. We parked outside of Blondie's house, about two blocks away. Dusk was coming on, but it was still warm.

I got out of the car, stretched for a minute, then took off down the road at a light jog. I was wearing blue tights and running shoes, a tight gray tank top and a fanny pack. A visor was helping to hold on a short black wig.

I stepped up the pace, wanting to have a nice glistening sheen of sweat on my chest when Blondie opened the door. Running this fast without a sports bra on was uncomfortable, and starting to hurt, but again, I wanted his eyes on my body and not on my face, on the off chance he recognized me. And so, a push-up bra.

I turned around and headed back. I was wearing earbuds in my ears and had what looked like an MP3 player strapped to my upper arm. It wasn't, though.

As I passed back by the parked car I flashed a thumbs-up to Ruby. She scowled back at me. She didn't like this plan any better than Marty did, but it stayed within the parameters I had set for this kind of operation. Only I went in, they provided technical, logistical, and getaway support. That was dangerous enough.

I jogged up the front steps of the townhouse, breathing heavily and sweating noticeably. And yes, my chest was heaving. The door was unlocked.

Chicago Blue

The building had been subdivided into three apartments, one on each floor. There were three buzzers. Number One said Baker, Dolores, on the first floor. Her mailbox was overflowing.

Apartment Two, on the second floor, didn't have a name, and Apartment Three had a *To Let* sign on it. I was betting on Apartment Two.

I jogged up the wooden stairs, making plenty of noise so that by the time I knocked on the door to Number Two it opened immediately. I didn't want to catch anyone by surprise.

He was still wearing his black suit pants and white shirt, but his jacket and tie were missing. He looked mildly surprised, his glance dropping almost immediately to check out my body.

"That your black Taurus out front?" I said to him in the extra-loud voice used by people wearing headphones.

"My car?" He said in surprise, his eyes still drawn to my chest.

"What?" I hollered.

"Huh?" he said, looking up.

"Oh, silly me," I said, removing the earbuds and unstrapping the black unit from my upper arm. "I can't hear a thing with these on." I held the black box in my left hand while I pointed down the stairs with my right. "Is that your black Taurus out there?"

He turned his head to look down the stairs and I shoved the stun gun into his gut, pushing hard on the trigger and shoving him back into his apartment without withdrawing my hand.

He tried to bat it away, but his motor skills were already failing. He tried to catch himself as he tripped backwards, but he fell heavily on his back with me straddling his chest.

Chicago Blue

I finally let go of the button. I didn't want him passing out. I set the stun gun down and pulled a roll of duct tape out of my fanny pack, pulling his hands onto his chest in front of me and taping them tightly. I stood and wrapped his ankles together as well. Only then did I stop to look around.

I closed the apartment door and locked it. We were in his kitchen, and a quick look revealed a living room, bathroom, and bedroom, all fairly tidy but reeking of cigarette smoke. Ugh. In the bedside table, I found an envelope with $3000 and his wallet. The license and credit cards all said Alan Watkins. I took them.

Back in the kitchen, I found his suit jacket hanging on the back of a kitchen chair, and beneath it his shoulder holster and automatic pistol. I took the pistol and tucked it into my fanny pack, which is where all the fashionable lady killers keep them. I shoved the money and wallet in there as well.

Alan had sat up and was trying to make his way toward the door. Drool was smeared across his cheek and he had wet his pants. I grabbed the back of his collar and tipped him back over, putting my sneakered foot on his neck. He brought his hands up instinctively to try and remove it, but I removed my foot and used my toe to kick him lightly in the nose.

"Oww!" he hollered, but I wasn't too worried about the noise, as it seemed the rest of the building was empty. I hopped back so that I was out of his reach, sat on the kitchen chair, and pulled off my visor and wig.

"So, Alan," I began.

"Riley?" he groaned with a mix of surprise and disgust. He started to edge toward me.

"Hold up right there, Alan," I warned. "I have your gun."

He stopped.

107

Chicago Blue

"I don't want any more moving or squirming, okay?"

"What the hell do you want?"

"Some answers. I've been wandering around the city like an idiot, hoping if I ask enough questions I'll figure out what the hell is going on. You keep popping up, so I was hoping you had some information I could use."

"I can't believe you're still in Chicago." He shook his head. "You must not have any common sense, whatsoever."

"Yeah, well, maybe not, but I'm not the one taped up on the floor." I gave him a disgusted look. "Don't they teach you the 'Sweaty Cleavage Diversion' at Bad Guy School?"

He had no decent response to this, so he just stared toward the door, wishing that one of us wasn't there.

"I'm not leaving until I find out who's trying to set me up. Is it Ralston?"

"Greg? I haven't talked to Greg in years."

"But he used to work for Fitzgerald, right?"

"Sure he did, but that was years ago. Besides, he's got his own security team now, he wouldn't have to hire us."

"Unless he didn't want anyone to know what he was doing."

"You think he blew up Blalock and Illcom? That's crazy, Farnham would obviously be the prime suspect, and Greg with him."

"Maybe crazy like a fox," I said. "So, who did hire you?"

"No idea."

"Right."

He shrugged.

"Seriously, above my pay grade, and I like it that way."

I considered this for a minute. Alan didn't seem like corner office material, so maybe he really didn't know.

Chicago Blue

"But if you don't know who hired you, how do you know it wasn't Ralston?" Aha!

"'Cause that would be stupid. He wouldn't do that."

"But you don't really know..."

He shifted his weight on the floor. Sitting in your own pee was probably pretty uncomfortable.

"No, I don't know for sure, but—"

"Shhh!"

"What?"

"Sssh! I thought I heard something."

We sat quietly for a moment, but there was nothing.

"Okay," I continued. "Why are you trying to kill me? You're not working for the police, that's for sure."

"We aren't trying to kill you—"

"You shot at me! Twice"

"No, just once."

"On Lakeshore Drive and at the salon."

"That was you at the salon?"

"Are you kidding me? You didn't know that was me?"

"Honestly, no. I always get thrown off by the hair."

Oh my god. I had been feeling smart for fooling this guy, but now I was doubting my accomplishment.

"You just shot at a random hairdresser?"

"No," he snorted. "I shot the window. I just wanted to scare her—you."

"Well, I feel so much better, but—" I paused again, and Watkins looked up at the ceiling. He had clearly heard something up there as well.

I drew the gun out of the fanny pack.

"Who's up there!" I hissed at him.

He just shrugged his shoulders.

I crept back through the apartment, checking each room and listening intently. I swung open the door to the bathroom. It was small and dim in the light of the one dirty window, and spoke clearly to the fact that a man

Chicago Blue

was the only current user. A bad smell, a layer of grime that would make me hesitant to touch any of the surfaces, an empty toilet paper roll in the dispenser.

Through the filmy window I suddenly saw a pair of legs come in to view, descending the fire escape. They were wearing black shiny latex.

Oh crap! I pulled the door shut quickly and raced back to the kitchen. She was like the Terminator and the Energizer Bunny mixed together. With a fetish model.

I grabbed a fistful of Watkins' hair, pulling his head way back.

"Who is she!" I rasped in his ear, holding the gun to his cheek. I heard the almost silent sound of the bathroom window sliding open. He grunted.

"She's who they brought in when we failed to get you the first time," he said, not bothering to keep his voice down.

I stepped to where I could see the bathroom door, and fired three bullets into it. The sound was deafeningly loud. From this angle, the bullets wouldn't hit someone on the other side of the door, but it would give them something to think about for a few seconds. I dropped the gun into Alan's lap and sprinted out the door and down the stairs.

She's who they call in...

Well, I hadn't been a secret agent very long, but I knew instinctively that, at least in this case, discretion was the better part of valor. I kept running.

As I pushed out the front door Ruby screeched to a halt at the end of the walk. She had heard the gunshots all the way up the block.

As much as I wanted to slide across the hood like a badass, I would most likely have slid off and cracked my head on the pavement. Instead I dove awkwardly, head first, through the open window of the rear passenger door.

"Go!" I shouted at Ruby, sitting up and turning to look back toward the townhouse.

She stood silhouetted against the lit doorframe, standing on the top step. I expected her to be holding a gun or, more likely, a crossbow or some crazy thing like that, but she appeared unarmed, her hands on her hips and her head cocked to the side, watching me. I smiled.

"Want a ride?" I yelled out the open window, but we were too far down the street to hear if she replied.

20

The next day I checked in to the Honeywell Retirement Lodge in Wilmette. Just for a visit.

"I'm here to read to Georgette Riley?" I said, holding up a copy of *Angela's Ashes* that I had picked up at Market Fresh Books. "I'm from the Senior Reads Program?"

The nurse at the desk was distracted, there seemed to be an issue with an older gentleman in cardiac arrest. She waved at a clipboard on the counter as she hurried away.

"Just sign in, please."

I entered my name as Jane Austen and then headed down the B wing to my mother's room. The place was clean but a bit threadbare. The framed prints on the wall, of works from the Art Institute, were so sun-faded you could barely make out some of them.

Once I was sure there were no police on site looking for me, I ducked into a restroom off the main hall. It had been more than eight weeks now since the bombing that started this whole mess, so it seemed unlikely that they would still be putting man hours into staking out my demented mother in hope of finding me. I knew a little bit about how they budgeted overtime, and I was pretty sure that by this time the Captain would be under pressure to scale back the hunt.

I took off the black wig I had worn at reception, and switched it for an auburn wig that looked, more or less, like my real hair used to look. I figured maybe today would be one of the rare days that my mother was lucid, in which case I didn't want to confuse her with my crewcut.

Looking in the mirror, it was comforting yet strange to see my old self again. Did I even know this person now? And if I wasn't that Kay Riley any more, then who was I? I shrugged and headed down the hall. That kind of introspection was going to have to wait until I had a little bit more free time.

My mother sat in an easy chair, watching *Wheel of Fortune* in her room. Her hair was not even white yet, mostly auburn with some streaks of gray, but here she was stuck for the rest of her life, surrounded by the elderly, her life gone away and left her.

"Hi, Mom," I said tentatively, and sat on the edge of her well-made bed. This place was modest, no doubt, but they did a pretty good job of keeping her room clean and tidy. I had no complaints, and if Mom did, well, she never said.

"Kay, it's you!" She beamed, and relief flooded me as I smiled back at her. I hadn't realized how much my heart had needed her to be present today, if only a little bit. I hadn't realized how desperate I was to be recognized. She looked to the door. "Where's your father?" she asked brightly. "Parking the car?"

"No, Mom. Dad couldn't make it today. It's just me."

"He never comes anymore, it seems." She frowned as a contestant on the screen landed on Bankrupt. I'm wasn't sure if she was frowning at that, or at Dad.

"He's busy, Mom."

"You have been, too," she said, smiling at me. "I've seen you on the nightly news!"

Uh oh.

"Oh that, Mom, well..."

"I'm so proud. My daughter, on the news! Some nice reporters even came and talked to me, to learn more about you for their newscast."

"I hope you didn't tell them anything embarrassing, Mom."

"Oh, no. Only good things. Like that time you played Peter Pan."

Chicago Blue

"That was third grade, Mom."

"You were such a little darling."

"Thanks, Mom."

A half-hour later she had dozed off while we were talking. I covered her with a blanket where she sat in the easy chair, reclining it a bit so her head wouldn't slump forward, then turned off the TV. I found a box of tissues and used them liberally. These visits always wore me out.

Then I got down to business. Her bookshelves held about 300 books—Mom had always been a great reader—and it took me a few minutes to find what I was looking for: Mom's address book.

Each year someone on the Honeywell's staff helped Mom send out Christmas cards, so I knew she must still have it. Most of the other memorabilia of our life as a family had come to me when Dad died, and was now sitting in a box under my bed.

I took the address book over to the window, where I could see better, and began thumbing through it. It was hard not to stop and think about each person as I saw their name. What were they thinking of me now? If I got caught, or killed, would they forever think that I had become a criminal, like my Uncle Patrick? That I hadn't followed in my father's footsteps after all?

It wasn't until near the back that I finally found what I was looking for. The listing was under the letter "S", but simply said, "Uncle E." and listed an address. No phone, no email.

I copied the address into my phone and put the book back in its place on the shelf. I switched out the red wig for the black one, picked up my book, and then leaned down and kissed my mother on the forehead.

"Bye, Mom," I said softly. "I'm going to fix this, I promise."

Chicago Blue

I sat in the parking lot in Ruby's borrowed car, searching through my satchel until I found what I was looking for: Aldo Frances's business card.

I had been thinking a lot about my conversation with Marty, and how much I was relying on him and Ruby, because I knew I could trust them. But now, as I began to look for Uncle Elgort, it occurred to me that there were several people on my side, and that maybe I didn't have to do everything by myself.

"Mr. Frances," I said, when he answered the phone. "It's Kay Riley. I have a question for you: Are you a Cubs fan or a White Sox fan?"

21

Uncle Elgort was probably somebody's uncle, but he wasn't mine. But that's what people in my dad's neighborhood had always called him. If Uncle Elgort asked you for a favor, you did him that favor. It was an unspoken understanding. Dad had bristled against this, knowing instinctively what those kind of connections led to, and so he made a point of moving out of the neighborhood soon after marrying Mom. His brothers, Patrick and Nicholas, however, did not.

Patrick, as I may have mentioned, went on to be a fairly hopeless car thief, and is still in jail to this day. I didn't mention that Nicholas, who became a very successful businessman, was close friends with Uncle Elgort's son Eldon. They attended Northwestern together, and had extensive business partnerships in the two decades afterward, until they were killed in a fire at their offices one horrible Easter Sunday.

Dad didn't take to Eldon, because of his father, and this had led to a frosty relationship between Uncle Nicholas and Dad. In fact, I only saw him at family holidays when I was a kid, and only met Eldon once or twice. I had never met Elgort. Not long after his son died, he retired from all his business holdings. He hadn't been a "person of interest" to the Chicago Police for years. It's unlikely they even knew where to find him these days— he would be a very old man at this point.

But Mom knew, because she had to make sure everyone got a Christmas card, come hell or high water.

The furniture shop was four stories tall, with three floors of showroom ("Three Amazing Floors of Bargains!!") and offices on the top floor.

I noticed the shatterproof glass in the front door as I entered, along with an overabundance of surveillance

Chicago Blue

cameras for a furniture store. A bell rang as the door closed behind me, and I hadn't gone more than a few feet before a strikingly handsome man, with graying temples and big brown eyes, stepped from between two wardrobes and greeted me warmly.

"Good afternoon, madam. Is there anything I can help you with?"

"Oh, not just at the moment," I said in a soft voice, pushing my glasses up on my nose. I was wearing a mousy brown wig, with a pale-yellow sweater over a white blouse. A black skirt and some conservative brown shoes rounded out my ensemble, along with a small brown purse. I would have felt safer wearing some of the excellent tactical gear I had bought using Alan Watkins's credit card, but it would have seemed a bit out of place in a furniture store, even one like this one.

"Well, I'm Don Shelby, one of the owners. You just find me if you need anything." He looked to be about 40, but he acted much older, and had the deep, tanned skin of someone who spent a lot of time on the golf course or on a yacht.

I cased the building carefully, while stopping every so often to try out a sofa or an easy chair. On the third floor, I spotted a door marked "Office" that wouldn't have attracted attention except for the fact that it looked very secure, and had a keypad lock. Set above it was yet another video camera, this one pointed straight at anyone who would be approaching.

I wandered slowly back down to the first floor until I found Don Shelby again, near the front door. He was intently studying his smartphone, and as I approached him from behind I could see that he was scrolling slowly through stock prices.

"Excuse me?"

Chicago Blue

He jumped a bit, and then turned toward me, putting on his best smile.

"Ah hello, I trust you found some excellent bargains during your tour. Is there something specific I can help you with?"

"Actually," I said, "no. Though it is all very lovely."

"Thank you."

"I was just, I was wondering. If you are one of the owners, I wonder if maybe you are related to an old friend of my parents, from ages ago."

His smile hardened just slightly.

"Perhaps," he answered in the same smooth tone. "Who is it you were looking for?"

"Uncle Elgort?"

His smile faltered for a moment, and he looked at me more closely, assessing, looking for any detail that would identify me as a threat.

"Hmmm," he said, recovering himself as he walked over to a multi-line phone that hung on the wall above an old roll top desk. "I haven't heard anyone use that name in a very long time."

He picked up the phone receiver and punched a button.

"Margaret? Yes, just checking, are we all clear on the sales floor? Yes? Okay, thanks. Go ahead with a one five then, would you?"

Shelby hung up and turned to me with a much more serious look on his face. The smile was gone. At the same time, I heard a loud click come from the front door.

Shelby started across the floor toward me, and I started for the door, knowing already that it was locked. And it was. I turned back to him with a bright, innocent smile on my face, but that clearly wasn't going to work because he was already pointing a revolver at me. It looked like an old Smith and Wesson.

Chicago Blue

I had been prepared for this, but it was still scary as hell. He gripped my arm above the elbow and dragged me around the corner and out of sight of the storefront windows.

Before I could twist around, or find any position from which I could conceivably disarm him, he pushed me roughly forward onto a bed. It had a lovely walnut headboard, but that wasn't my top priority right now. I started to roll over.

"Stay," he warned, with a knee in my back. I stayed, though it was infuriating to not be able to see him. I started to raise my head, but he pushed it back down. He ran his hand down my back and under my arms, and then up my skirt.

"Whoa, fella," I quipped.

"Be quiet," he suggested, removing his hand.

I started to raise my head again, and he grabbed it again, so roughly that my wig came off, revealing my red buzz cut. Shelby grunted in surprise. I heard him step back, then I heard the contents of my handbag spill onto the floor.

He grunted again.

"Who is this person who claims to be a friend of Uncle Elgort?"

"Georgette Riley. My mother. Georgette. Riley."

He sat down on the edge of the bed.

"We'll see," he said, as he roughly pulled my hands behind my back and cuffed me with my own police handcuffs, which had spilled out of my bag.

He strode around the corner, back to where the phone was, and I heard him talking in low tones. I suppose I could have made a run for it, but I really wanted to talk to Uncle Elgort, so I just lay there and wallowed in the special self-pity that comes from being restrained with your own handcuffs.

Chicago Blue

Shelby came back into the room and gathered my things from the floor, putting them back in my handbag.

"Get up," he said.

Well, I tried, but I had no leverage on the soft bed and ended up rolling off it on to the floor. I popped right back up however, intent on looking like a competent professional.

He picked the wig up off the bed and stuffed it in the purse as well.

"Follow me."

"Can you uncuff me, please?"

"No, I can't."

Okey-dokey then. We headed upstairs through a forest of lamps and dressers and then up another flight until we stood in front of the door I had noticed earlier. Don shielded the keypad with his hand while I gave my best smile to the camera. The door clicked open and we entered a dark hallway that led to a flight of stairs. At the top of the stairs was another door with another keypad, and then we were in what looked like the waiting room of a very upscale lawyer's office. Antique furniture, deep carpet, an unoccupied reception desk.

We went through a big oak door on the far side of the room. Surprisingly, this led to a large, airy loft that took up the rest of the fourth floor. I had expected a smoky office of some kind. Instead, there were worktables, cubicles, a photographic studio and racks of clothing.

As we crossed the room, an old man came out from behind one of the dividers. He wore a full three-piece suit, which was crazy because who did that nowadays? He had an expensive-looking watch and nicely shined leather shoes. His head was bald on top with a fringe of neat gray around the sides and back, and he had a little gray mustache. I'd guess he was about eighty based on the wrinkles and sagging skin, but he carried himself well and his brown eyes were large and bright. They widened when they saw me, scanning the incongruous contrast of my punk hair and my Susie-Q housewife outfit.

"You're Kay Riley?" he asked, in a soft, ironic voice that suggested he already knew all about me.

I straightened up. "I am."

"How is your father these days?"

"He's dead, has been for 12 years. You sent flowers."

"And your Uncle Patrick, do you visit him often?"

"He's in Florida."

He raised his eyebrows.

"Yes," I said. "A transfer for work. I don't see him very often at all."

"What kind of work?" the old man inquired.

"Corrections," I deadpanned.

"Does he enjoy that?"

"Mostly, but he doesn't get out much."

His eyes twinkled, but I was losing my patience with his little tests.

"I had another uncle," I pressed. "Whom I believe was partners with your son."

A pained look crossed his face.

"Yes," he replied, in a much more dour tone. "That is why you have been permitted to meet with me. That," and here he smiled again, "and the fact that your mother sends me a Christmas card every year."

"I'm afraid she hasn't been well for some time." Now it was my turn to be dour.

"I know, I know. But a lovely woman. Obviously, your father never saw eye to eye with the boys, but your mother was always so kind, and believed so strongly in family."

"I need some help," I blurted out.

Chicago Blue

"I know. Come," he indicated a dining table surrounded by comfortable-looking chairs. He opened my purse, which Don had left on the table, and rooted around in it until he found my handcuff keys. He moved slowly back around the table toward me, and I turned away so that he could undo the cuffs. Well, that was progress at least.

He sat down heavily at the table and motioned me to do the same.

"Eldon will bring us some refreshment, and you will tell me your whole story, though I'm not sure what I can do. I do not have the same influence in the city that I had as a younger man."

An hour later, he knew everything that I knew. I'm sure he knew a lot more, but he wasn't the type of person who shared information easily. After bringing us lemonade, Don, or Eldon—named for his uncle, I guessed—sat down and joined us, occasionally scratching a note on a legal pad.

"Well, my dear. That is indeed a pickle," Elgort said kindly. "I see why you thought I might be able to help, and perhaps I can. Our family has long since ceased involvement with most of the criminal element in Chicago. We concern ourselves mostly these days with financial institutions, which is just a better class of criminal, to be honest. But quieter, safer. And, furniture, of course," he smiled, indicating the room around him. "However, for the right people and the right price, there are certain artistic endeavors that we specialize in."

I shifted uncomfortably in my seat.

"Payment is going to be a problem."

Don snorted, like he had expected as much, but Uncle Elgort just took a sip of lemonade and then gently set the glass onto the table.

"I don't want you to worry about that, dear," he said.

Chicago Blue

I knew what was coming, the old, "Sometime in the future I will need a favor from you" line. I was prepared for it, but I didn't like it. This was exactly how people got pulled into organized crime. An offer you can't refuse, as they say. Still, I needed what I needed, and my situation wasn't getting any better. I believe there's an old Czech saying that goes: "When you find yourself in a hole, first stop digging." That's easily said, but right now, it seemed that digging was the only way out.

But Uncle Elgort surprised me.

"I owe your uncle many debts," he said. "And your mother too, for that matter. Neither of whom I can repay, so you, Miss Riley, will be the lucky recipient of their due. Just this once."

"Thank you, Uncle Elgort."

He turned to Don.

"Get Nicky, would you?"

Don got up at once and headed toward the back of the loft, disappearing behind some large wooden crates. I smiled nervously and sipped my lemonade, not sure what kind of small talk would be appropriate.

"Quite a little mess you've gotten yourself into," Uncle Elgort chuckled.

"Wrong place, wrong time, I guess."

"Opportunity appears in strange guises." He leaned forward and raised his glass again. "Or, to put it in more prosaic terms: When life gives you lemons..." and he took a drink.

I was saved having to respond to this truism by the appearance of a man from around the crates where Don had disappeared.

I did a double take. It was as if Don had stepped into a time machine and gone backward 10 years. This younger version was thinner, with no gray in his hair, and was a lot paler. Same handsome face though, sharp nosed with dark eyebrows over large brown eyes, with lots of wavy dark hair and black-framed glasses that made him look far more bookish than Don.

"Ah," said Elgort. "There you are. This is my other nephew, Nick. This is Miss Kay Riley—it is still Miss, is it not?"

I nodded, then also nodded at Nick. He was a very good-looking guy, but he also looked like he didn't get out in the sun or the fresh air much. He wore tan chinos and a denim shirt that had flecks of paint all over it. His hands, which were long-fingered and very attractive—what? I like hands—also had traces of paint on them. For some reason, he was barefoot.

"Miss Riley needs a full set, Nicky, and she needs it right away."

"Judging from the TV news, I'd say you're right about that." His voice was softer and warmer than his brother's—for they were clearly brothers—but still had a crisp efficiency to it, as if he would perhaps rather be doing something else.

"Yes, indeed," agreed Uncle Elgort. "Can you take care of it now?"

"Of course, Uncle."

"Very good." Elgort put both palms on the table and pushed himself up to a standing position. He turned to me.

"I'm sorry it's been so long, and we don't really know each other, my dear. But your father..."

"Yes, my father. I can imagine."

"Anyway, strange bedfellows, as they say. I am happy to meet you now, and hear about your great adventure, but I must attend to some business. You are in good hands with Nicholas."

"Thank you, sir."

Chicago Blue

And with that, he ambled across the room to a freight elevator, Don at his side, and a moment later descended out of sight.

After Uncle Elgort was gone, Nicholas looked me over from head to foot. I smiled my best smile. He sighed.

"You can't have that hair," he said, waving vaguely at my red head.

"But it's the only hair I've got," I said, coyly, then stopped myself. "No wait, I've got some in here." I grabbed my bag and pulled out the matted wig I had worn earlier. It looked like a chinchilla that someone had run through a blender.

"That won't do," Nick said. "Come with me."

I followed him across the room to where a large, white screen was set up, along with cameras and lights. To the right were racks of clothing and several dressers. On top of the dressers, Styrofoam heads wore a selection of wigs.

Nick looked at me again, studying my face, and then reached for a wig made of long, jet black hair. "Try this."

I did. It looked amazing. The hair was long and wavy and full of luster, clearly of a better quality than the party store wigs I had been wearing. Nick stepped closer to me and adjusted the wig on my head, smoothing it down around the temples and behind the ears. He was about six feet tall, and standing this close I found myself examining the paint stains on his shirt. There were at least a dozen different colors.

"Are you building something colorful?" I asked.

He looked down and followed my sight line.

"I paint pictures," he said, nonchalantly, "though I often am called on to paint or draw other things." I looked up at him, and he licked his finger and used it to smooth down the hairline of the wig. I wasn't sure if that was erotic or disgusting. I guess things like that can depend on who is doing them.

126

Chicago Blue

"I'm not a messy painter," he added, stepping back from me. "This is just my favorite work shirt. I've had it for years."

He turned me toward the mirror and I gasped.

"It's amazing."

"It's important to match the skin tone," he said. "We can't go with your normal color, because then you'll look too much like yourself. Which, of course, is normally what you would want, because now you are going to have to wear this wig every time you have to use this ID."

"That's going to be a pain."

"Well, I'll make you another set if you live through the end of July. One that looks just like you, but with a different name."

He had been kidding, I think, but the brutality of his statement caught me off guard, and I felt fear and pain welling in my chest. I was so distracted that I thought I heard him tell me to take off my shirt.

"What?"

"I said take off your shirt."

"Man, you really know how to treat a girl."

"We need a different outfit, for the picture. Something more sophisticated."

"Now I'm unsophisticated, too. Great. At least I'll be dead soon." I started pulling hard at the buttons of my sweater, fighting to keep angry so I wouldn't start crying.

"Woah, woah, woah." He put both hands up in surrender. "You're right. That was a terrible thing to say." He dropped his hands and turned toward a rack of clothes. "I was annoyed at getting called away from my regular work." He pulled out a light gray silk shirt that looked like it would be fantastic under a business suit. "And, I guess I'm used to dealing with slightly more hardened criminals. I forgot your situation."

127

Chicago Blue

"I'm hard enough," I sneered, and I pulled my blouse off my shoulders and threw it to the ground.

I'd learned my lesson on Belinda Blalock's fence, and was wearing much more impressive underwear today. The bra was still white, but it had some lace to it and pushed me up in the right places. I wouldn't want to do calisthenics in it, but it looked great, and was just right for showing some jerk how tough you were, unembarrassed to be stripping down in front of a stranger. Hardened? This guy looked like he hadn't even gone *outside* in a decade. Don't give me hardened.

Nicholas turned away, reddening. "The skirts fine," he said. "It's not going to show."

I pulled the shirt roughly from his outstretched hand and put it on. It fit beautifully, and the string of pearls he handed me looked elegant yet businesslike against my neck.

He walked to a dresser and opened the top drawer, gesturing me toward him. He pulled out a makeup set and began applying foundation to my face.

Was I too shiny?

He read my thoughts. "This is to cover your freckles and darken your complexion a bit." He pulled out a very light brown pencil and started to draw small lines from the corners of my eyes. "I'm also aging you up about a decade. This is very effective, but it needs to be simple— if I give you the makeup do you think you can replicate it?"

"Yeah, I think I'm simple enough to handle it." Now I was just being a jerk. But I hold a grudge. "Why are you making me look older?"

"Age is one of the factors that sticks in an eyewitness's mind. People unconsciously categorize and sort. We want you to be in a different category, so their mind doesn't make the connection between the new you and the old you. If they are looking for someone who is twenty-five, they will gloss right past someone who is forty."

"I'm thirty-three."

"Really? I would have said for sure you were mid-twenties."

Grudge, officially gone.

He ushered me over to the white screen, and took some basic mug shot, DMV-type photos. Then he brought me over a red sweater and white t-shirt.

"Change into these," he said, as he proceeded to roll up the white screen, revealing a bright green one underneath.

This time I turned away from him as I changed. I pulled the t-shirt carefully over my head, mindful of the wig and makeup, and put the sweater on.

Nick came up behind me and drew my fake hair into a ponytail, holding it with a clip. He handed me a pair of glasses to put on, and had me stand in front of the green screen, in several poses. Then I took off the sweater and we repeated the process.

"Okay," Nick said, standing up from the camera and stretching his back. "Let's just get your fingerprints and we'll be done."

"Fingerprints?"

"For your police record."

"I don't have a police record."

"Sure you do," he smiled. "Georgette Wrigley, arrested for refusing to co-operate with a police officer. During the Women's March. It's my favorite little touch. People who make up new identities never think to add things like arrests. I usually do a drunk driving charge, or shoplifting, but since you are a virtuous civil rights attorney the march seems like a great fit."

"But I'm a police officer. My prints are already on file."

He smiled at me like I was a babe in the woods.

Chicago Blue

"I think my brother Eldon is already taking care of that."

I raised my eyebrows. "He better be an outstanding hacker if he is going to get into the police department."

"That's not necessary. Sometimes it's just a matter of knowing the right people if you want something to be accidentally deleted."

"And the Shelby family knows the right people?"

"Still."

I stepped behind the rack of clothes and removed the costume items, hanging them back on the rack and putting my own clothes back on.

"Georgette Wrigley?"

"Sure. You want your alias to be easy to remember, so that you aren't stumbling over it. You're not a White Sox fan, are you?"

I stepped out from behind the rack and smiled at him.

"No, Cubbies all the way."

"Then we're good."

22

"Elgort Shelby!"

"Ruby, I—"

"Elgort Fucking Shelby! I do not *believe* you!"

"Look, I just..." but Ruby had stomped off, limping over to the picnic table and plopping down on one of the benches.

We were in the grassy park area outside my safe house. She had taken more than an hour to drive here, doubling back repeatedly to make sure she wasn't followed. I had insisted on more stringent protocol since realizing a very talented, possibly psychotic assassin was on my trail. None of us would be safe if she was able to track Ruby or Marty to me.

I walked over to Ruby, but instead of sitting at the picnic table I laid down on my back in the grass, about five feet away. I looked up at the big puffy clouds moving slowly across the blue morning sky. The short blades of grass tickled against my crew cut. I was tired, and the more I rested, the more tired I got, which is probably a definition of depression right there. I wanted to be out and doing something, anything to help my case. I didn't want to be having this argument with Ruby. I watched the silhouette of a bird float lazily across my vision.

Ruby's voice came to me quietly.

"Have I ever told you what happened to my knee?"

I sighed audibly. "Yes. Yes you have. Two story fall in a carpark during a pursuit."

"It was Two Thousand—"

"—Two, I know."

"It was Marco Colatano."

I raised my head to look at her, but she was staring off into space.

"What?"

Chicago Blue

"The Colatanos. You know of them, yes?"

"Of course, everyone does."

"They were extorting protection money from a variety of businesses in my precinct. Captain Earl was furious. I mean, pfft, protection money? That went out in the Seventies, right? Well, apparently not.

"I had taken the place of one of Sal Tomaso's waitresses. I would deliver the payment at the agreed-upon spot, I'd have a wire. Other agents would be hidden in cars throughout the car park. Everyone knew the payoffs took place at the car park. Colatano might as well have had a sign out front." She sighed. "That was the whole strategy, yes? The brazenness. Nobody would ever squeal, because their whole family would be killed. Well, Sal Tomaso squealed. Brave or stupid, who knows."

I propped myself up on my elbows so I could look up at Ruby as she told the story.

"There was usually only Colatano at the pick-up, he liked to do these things himself, but we brought half a dozen cops, just to be safe. You know the saying, *You come for the King, don't miss the King.*"

"Something like that," I said.

"Well, Tomaso's life was on the line. And, this was going to be the big takedown that Captain Earl had been waiting for. So very important, very tense. Your father was there that day, too."

"What? You never told me that!"

She shrugged. "It never came up. We worked together a lot in those days. He was a good guy, and he didn't like mobsters," she added pointedly.

"What happened?"

"I don't know. They made the whole unit. I'm not sure how. Somebody must have talked. It's likely Colatano had people inside the force."

Chicago Blue

Hmm. I thought about what Nick had said about the Shelby's ability to access police files by knowing the right people.

"I came out of the elevator. Boom. They have a knife to my throat. Colatano's not there, because of the tip off. It's two of his guys. They search me, not gently I can tell you. They find the wire and that's it, Earl calls it and everyone rushes the scene. Like I said, there's only two of them, and about six cops, so then Colatano's guy, Mike Minneola, he's using me as a human shield while his partner, Stevie Guigino jumps behind a car and starts firing on anyone who shows their face.

"Minneola, he knows time is not on his side in a situation like this—they've got limited bullets and nowhere to go, he's backed up to a guard rail with no easy way out—he's trying to slide sideways back toward the elevator while Guigino is keeping them busy. Basically leaving Guigino to fend for himself. The cops are all jumpy, because now they know it's a setup. Maybe there's more men hiding, maybe a bomb. Who knows?"

I've sat all the way up by this time, hanging on Ruby's every word.

"I catch Earl's eye," she continues. "He's about 30 feet away, behind some big pickup truck. We give each other a look. He nods. I show him my hand with three fingers extended. He nods. Two. One. I grab Minneola's hand and pull down and turn, dragging him around until he's between me and the captain. Before he can react, the captain shoots him three times in the back."

"Oh my god!" I gasp. "What happened?"

She shrugged.

"Good plan, bad execution. The force of the shots pushed Minneola, and me with him, over the railing and down onto the level below. He hit the cement, and I landed on top of him," she slapped her hand on the

133

picnic table for emphasis, "or I would be dead now, too. My left leg was stretched out to the side as we went down, and it clipped the roof of a car, wham. Bye bye knee joint."

"Ooph," I said, feeling sick to my stomach.

"Ooph indeed," agreed Ruby. "So, you see my point?"

"Actually, no. Why are you telling me this?"

"The next day, Sal Tomaso's house explodes. Gas leak. He's dead, along with his wife and two kids."

"That's terrible!"

"Elgort Shelby. Marco Colatano. Same thing."

"But he's—"

"No 'but'!" said Ruby fiercely. "There are no good mobsters. Like the hooker with the gold heart. Not real. I know this has been hard for you, Kay. I do," she went on, talking over my objection. "But it's making you a little crazy. A little wild. The means are not justified—"

"By the ends?" I stood up and put my hands on my hips. "That's easy for you to say. What happens to me if I get caught? You think they'll just suddenly realize their mistake? C'mon Ruby. You know how this works. Close cases, as quickly as you can. That's how they operate."

"We will figure this out. Together," Ruby said in a voice that sounded like pleading.

"And if we can't?" I put my hand on her shoulder, trying to show that I was not mad, but that I was unmoved. "If I have to leave the country, can you get me fake documents?"

Ruby exhaled so long and mournfully that I thought she might deflate completely into a crumpled mess on the ground.

"I'm just worried about you."

I gave her a hug.

"I'm worried about me too, but if there ever *was* a case of the means justifying the ends, this is it."

Chicago Blue

"I'm not agreeing with you, officially," Ruby said, straightening up. "I'm just not actively disagreeing for the time being."

That seemed to be as good as I was going to get.

"Great," I said, pulling out my phone and looking at the time. "I've got to go inside and get suited up for the ball game. We've got to leave in fifteen minutes."

23

Wrigley Field. One of my dad's favorite places in the world. I used to sit next to him in section 108 and read. Harry Potter and, forgive me, those Lurlene McDaniel books where there's always a kid dying. I'd look up when everyone cheered. Otherwise, I was in my own world.

I felt a bit bad about it now; I'm sure Dad had wished I was really into it, he loved the Cubbies so much.

It was a beautiful afternoon, sunny with a light breeze. The smell of ballpark food wafted my way as I sat down next to an older man wearing a Cubs cap low over his eyes, and oddly, a silk scarf that obscured part of his face.

"That's your idea of a disguise?"

Aldo Frances looked over at me and did a double take. I was in my full Georgette Wrigley look, accessorized with dark glasses, a stylish black silk shirt, and my leather pants. I looked glamorous, which you wouldn't think would be a good disguise, especially at a ball game, but I looked so different from my old self (who would have worn jeans and a Cubs sweatshirt) that it worked like a charm. Georgette Wrigley, Wrigley Field. Heck, maybe I owned the place. Nicholas was right: it's an easy name to remember.

"Miss Riley, my goodness, what a transformation!"

"Thanks. I wish I could say the same about you. Nobody wears a scarf to a ballgame, Aldo."

"On the other hand," he replied, "I've never been to a baseball game in my life, so it is very unlikely that anyone will be looking for me here."

"Great, then I picked a good spot."

"Are the Cubs a good team?" he asked.

"Sure," I said distractedly. "All they need is some good hitting, some better pitching, and a little bit of fielding practice and they'll have the pennant."

Chicago Blue

"Huh?"

"Nothing, just something my Dad used to say. The Cubs are great. They won the title last year and it only took them 100 tries."

I was staring across the field to the seats behind the first-base line, where Ruby was sitting watching me through binoculars. I lowered my sunglasses and winked at her, then raised them back up. It was hard for Ruby and I to stay mad at each other. What she had said to me stung, because parts of it were dead on, but she only said them because she loved me.

"Have you found anything out, Miss Riley?" asked Frances, interrupting my train of thought.

"Not as much as I'd like, that's why I contacted you. I'm hitting some dead ends."

"Well, perhaps together we can make some headway. I've heard absolutely nothing from the police."

The park turned out to be a good meeting place. There was no one seated next to Frances, and the woman on my other side was really into the game, and into her boyfriend, who was seated on the other side of her. There was a constant buzz of white noise, punctuated by cheers or groans. Aldo related to me his experience with the police while I kept my eye on Ruby, to make sure she was continuing to show the all-clear sign. If anyone in my section did anything suspicious, she would let me know by taking off her hat.

He knew all about my visit to Belinda Blalock, from the news, but was surprised at my success in hunting down Alan Watkins. He chuckled.

"You are very ingenious, my dear. But this is all a bit dangerous, isn't it? Who would have thought our lives would lead us to this?" He sighed. "This news about Greg Ralston's old company is disturbing. Both Ferris and Carter have known Ralston for a long time."

Chicago Blue

"You talk like you know Ferris well also."

"Fairly well."

"But he's your main competitor!"

"Ah," the older man said. "You make it sound so simple. As I mentioned before, Carter and Ferris were still very good friends. They kept it secret from the public, because they were constantly afraid of being accused of collusion, or anti-trust behavior."

He turned more toward me, leaning closer.

"It is rumored, and I have been investigating this in great detail, that there was some kind of agreement between the two of them, regarding a merger, or some sort of stock deal, if anything ever happened to the other. Did you find out anything about that?"

"Belinda Blalock told me that she holds no financial interest in Illcom, at all."

"Well, that would fit."

"And Arthur Vincente, the Chair of the Illcom board. Do you think he knew about this?"

"I don't know, and I can't find out. Arthur is still in the hospital under heavy sedation. When I visited him, he was unconscious the entire time I was there."

"Yes. I'm afraid that is looking like a permanent diagnosis."

"That's terrible!"

"It doesn't make sense, it can't be one of them," I grumbled. "If it was Farnham, he wouldn't have sent a live bomb into his own building."

"Also," Aldo added, "if Ferris has some sort of claim to Illcom, then why hasn't he made a move? It's been weeks since Carter died."

"Wait a minute!" I sat up in excitement. The Cardinals pitcher gave up a double and the crowd roared. "Catwoman!"

"I beg your pardon?"

Chicago Blue

I quickly told him about my new friend, the snappy dresser who climbs through ceilings and bathroom windows. As you can imagine, he was intrigued.

"You say she stole a piece of paper from Farnham's office?"

"Yes! This could be the connection. But who is she? And why is she following me now? And how?"

"Do you have a cell phone now," Aldo asked.

"Of course, but it's just a burner phone. I got rid of my old phone."

"Still, someone could be tracing you."

"How is that possible?"

"My dear, use your head. You are smack in the middle of a conspiracy involving the leaders of the telecommunications industry. They've got quite a bit of technology at their disposal, some of which I designed myself. They could be monitoring anyone you've ever known, anyone you're related to, waiting for you to call them. Once you do, they've got your new number."

I smacked myself on the forehead. How could I have been so stupid? I was worried about putting Ruby and Marty in danger, but they'd been in danger the whole time. And it was my fault.

While I was self-flagellating, Aldo had taken out his cell phone and made a call. He spoke to someone in a hushed voice for a few minutes, and I tried to nonchalantly eavesdrop. I had no luck with that, so I flagged down a vendor and got myself a pretzel. Across the way Ruby was still watching, her cap still firmly on her head.

Aldo hung up.

"So," he began. "I have some good news and some bad news."

"Yes?" I asked with my mouth full.

Chicago Blue

"At Illcom we have our own security department as well. As acting CEO, I'm just beginning to find out how effective it is. I have the name of someone who fits the description of your mystery woman."

"Really? That's amazing."

"Her name is Selena Salerno, and she is known throughout the Chicago underworld. My source tells me that it is believed that she is currently working for Pershing Industrial."

"That's great! What's the bad news?"

"She is incredibly dangerous. From what I've been told, you are very, very lucky to be alive. I think you should come with me, right now. We can keep you safe and hidden until this is resolved."

"It's been a pretty hair-raising few weeks," I admitted, "but I think it's better if I stay solo. Isn't Pershing a pharmaceutical company?"

"Not only. They have their hand in anywhere they think they can make a dollar, and they have a long record of unscrupulous activity. Unfortunately, the current government administration cares little about such behavior. I wouldn't be at all surprised if Pershing were looking to get into telecom."

I was incredulous.

"But they can't just blow up the CEOs of the two leading companies and waltz in and take over, even in this day and age..."

"No," Aldo agreed. "But they might wait a year, or two. They are in it for the long game. Or, given the hit that Farnham's stock has taken, they might try for a hostile takeover."

I finished my pretzel. Selena Salerno. At least I had a name now. At least she was real, and not some twisted product of my imagination.

Chicago Blue

"You didn't see what the paper she took said?" asked Aldo.

"What?"

"The document that the Salerno woman took. Did you see it?"

"Not close enough to make out any words."

"A pity, it might have told us what Pershing's plan was. Give me your phone."

"What?" I had been lost in my own thoughts. Aldo held out his hand.

"Your phone."

I handed it to him. He removed the SIM card and dropped it on the cement by his feet, crushing it with the heel of his shoe.

He pulled his own phone out, removed the card, and put it into my phone.

"What does that do?" I asked, taking my phone back.

"It is untraceable. I designed it myself. If they have been tracking your phone, then this will make you much safer."

"But wait, isn't this your phone number? How does that work?"

Aldo laughed, in a way that made me feel like a stupid child.

"This is just the card I use for secure calls." He pulled another one out and slid it into the phone. "This is the one I use for business."

Hmph. Learn something new every day.

I looked away from him and across the field, where I noticed Ruby removing her cap and putting it back on again, over and over. I crumpled up my pretzel wrapper and stood up, looking around. At the top of the ramp, about 50 yards away, I saw one of the jerks that had been with Watkins at the hair salon. I sat back down, quickly.

Chicago Blue

"Mr. Frances, we've got company."

He instinctively made to stand, but I grabbed his arm and pulled him back down again.

"Be careful," I hissed. "They must have traced my phone here, like you said, but they won't know exactly where we are, and they won't likely recognize me."

Frances pulled out his phone, but I stopped him.

"Help isn't going to get here in time, unless your security is sitting right outside."

He shook his head no.

"Listen, you should stay here, and I will leave quickly and quietly."

I looked across the field to see that Ruby was no longer in her seat. She was on her way up the steps and out of the stadium, her phone pressed to her ear. Hopefully, she was calling our chauffeur.

"But Miss Riley, it could be me that they are after. What should I do?"

"You? Why you?"

"Think about it. Carter Blalock is dead and Arthur Vincente is nearly so. That leaves me in charge of everything at Illcom. If someone is trying to destroy the company, I could be next."

"Right, of course."

"I think we should stick together here and call my security detail," Aldo said.

I wasn't keen on that idea. I looked around for an answer, and spotted the pretzel vendor coming up the steps at the end of the row. "Listen. Keep your head down, and when this guy with the tray comes by, follow him very closely up the steps. Right behind him."

"Okay."

"When you get to the first walkway, turn right, and then head down the tunnel and out. Keep your hat low. I'll be right behind you."

Chicago Blue

He did as I told him, and a few moments later we were climbing the steps. I chanced a look toward our friend. He was still there, scanning the crowd. I decided to take my chances. He had only ever seen me in the salon, with pink hair and fake tattoos. Georgette Wrigley was going to be able to walk right past him.

And that's exactly what I did. Instead of turning right, I went up an additional set of stairs until I was on his level, then moved right on by, leaving behind only a pretzel wrapper and a smashed phone card. Take that, bad guys!

I skipped down the ramp and out into the street, where I saw Aldo getting safely into his chauffeured car. The weather was beautiful, and I felt oddly free in my disguise. I could get used to Georgette Wrigley. She wore great clothes, and she wanted to save the world. Nothing wrong with that.

Marty pulled up in his car, with Ruby in the passenger seat. I opened the door and hopped in the back seat.

"What now?" asked Marty.

"Let's go to Del Campo's and have tacos on the beach."

"That's crazy," said Ruby.

"I don't care. Let's celebrate being alive!"

"I'm with you," said Marty and pulled into traffic.

"I disapprove," said Ruby.

"Want us to drop you off somewhere?" I asked.

"Are you kidding. My sister Clara would never forgive me if something happened to Martin. I'm not letting you two out my sight. And," she added. "I really like those deeply-fried burritos."

"Chimichangas?" asked Marty.

"If you say so. Let's go."

And we did. And it was glorious.

24

The next day I was rocking the Wrigley disguise again, looking exactly like a civil rights lawyer on her lunch break. Business suit and briefcase, low heels, fashionable glasses. I ran my hand through my raven tresses, as I liked to call them, and checked my look in the rearview mirror of my rental car. I was running a close surveillance job on a professional, so it was important that my disguise was perfect.

It occurred to me that I should really get a motorcycle if I was going to be doing a lot of this kind of work in the future. The parking, the flexibility, the fact that I'd always wanted one. Then I realized, for the millionth time, that I could be in jail or dead any day now. Not really the time to think about long-term purchases. A little red one would be awesome.

I was able to rent a car, a nondescript Ford Taurus, thanks to Uncle Elgort and his great-nephew, Nicholas. Last night I had returned to Shelby Furniture after Nick emailed to tell me my documents were ready.

Uncle Elgort had been nowhere around, but Don had met me at the door and escorted me to a back office on the ground floor, away from the showroom windows.

He had me take a seat and then buzzed upstairs for Nicholas. While we were waiting, he leaned back in his chair and gave me a long look.

"I think we met, once," he said at last.

"Really?"

"Yes. I know your Dad didn't want anything to do with our family—"

I started to object, but he waved me away.

"Don't worry, I don't hold it against you, as I was about to say, you were a little girl. Not your fault. But I'm pretty sure you were one of the kids at Eldon and

Chicago Blue

Nicholas's funeral. You and Nicky are barely old enough to remember it, but you were both there." His faced soured. "It was a terrible day."

"You're named for him?"

"I am." He offered no more, and we sat in silence for a minute until Nicholas entered the office, a manila folder in his hand.

"Well, looks like you two are getting along just great," he said, setting the folder on the desk.

"Hello."

He looked at me.

"Stand up and take the glasses off, if you don't mind."

I did as he asked, suddenly a bit self-conscious. He stepped close and peered at my face.

"Nice work with the make-up. You've done it just as I showed you."

"Yes, sensei."

He ignored me, probing my hairline to check that I had attached the wig properly. He stepped back.

"Looks good," he nodded. "You might want to be a little more careful with your cleavage."

I looked down. I had the top two buttons of my blouse undone, but I wouldn't call it indecent by *any* stretch of the imagination.

"The freckles," he said hastily. "They don't match your new complexion. You should put some base on them."

I looked down at my chest, and then realized he was looking at my chest as well. Then he realized that I realized that he was looking at my chest, and we both reddened and looked away at the same time.

"Okay!" said Don, rising to his feet and clapping his hand together. "I'll let you two have some time alone."

Nick and I began to protest at the same time, but Don had already left the room.

Chicago Blue

Silence hung in the air for a moment, and then I motioned with my eyes toward the folder on the desk.

"Yes," he said, recovering. "Here we are."

He started at the beginning. Birth certificate, high school transcripts (I could have done better, if I'd only dedicated myself to studying a little harder). Driver's license, two credit cards, a passport. Lastly there were three wallet-sized photos. One of me with two little girls, one of me standing in front of the Taj Mahal, and one of my father and mother and me when I was 6 years old.

The first two were fakes, made with the photos he took in front of the green screen (I have no idea who the little girls were, but I've since named them Hazel and Maria, my nieces). The third photo was the real thing, and I looked up at Nicholas with astonishment.

"How? Where did you get this?"

"Mom. She hoarded family memorabilia, there's boxes of it."

I frowned. "She's passed?"

"Yeah, Dad too. It's just me and Don and Uncle Elgort, who seems prepared to live to 150. Anyway," he stepped around to the back of the desk and sat down, "that must be from a wedding of one of the cousins. Don says weddings and wakes were about the only thing your family showed up for."

I looked at the picture again, and had to swallow back tears.

"Thank you. I don't have many pictures like this."

"I'm glad you like it."

I rose to leave, gathering everything back into the manila folder and putting it in my shoulder bag.

"Will you send me an invoice?"

Nick smiled.

"I'm sure you know it doesn't work like that." He straightened up quickly when he saw my expression change. "I don't mean anything sinister," he rushed to add. "It's just Uncle Elgort. He made it clear there was to be no charge."

"Well," I stopped with my hand on the door. "Tell him I said thank you, and I will pay him back some day."

So now I was able to rent a car, and buy things with a credit card (Don had set up a bank account for me with $5000 in it, and a PO box in my new name for the bills to go to).

It was a big, big help, and if I needed to get out of the city, or out of the country, fast, I'd be able to do it now. But I couldn't leave yet. I was determined to clear my name, or at least figure out who had framed me, and get some revenge.

That's why I was on surveillance detail, and just across the street I could see my target getting out of his car: Greg Ralston.

He stepped quickly from the car and entered the building. I checked my hair in the rearview one last time, grabbed my lunch bag, and followed.

25

Illcom and Frandling. It seemed like there were a lot more connections between the two companies than most people realized. In fact, looking back through press coverage over the last decade, it was rare to find any instances of the two companies attacking each other in public. Sure, they had competing phone and internet plans, but it did not seem as hostile as Coke and Pepsi, or McDonalds and Burger King. Katy Perry and Taylor Swift. No lawsuits, no acrimony. Two companies in the same field, headquartered in the same city, run by two men who had been college pals. Hmm.

I was beginning to think that the stolen document might dictate the terms of a merger, if one of the two men were to die or be incapacitated. This would be highly unusual, as both Farnham and Illcom were public companies, but each CEO did own more than 50% of their respective companies.

So many connections, and one of them was Greg Ralston. Not only that, be he had been in the building the night of the first bombing, and hadn't been very helpful when it came to saving Carter Blalock.

I was convinced that I was on the right track with Ralston. I had followed as he left work mid-day, driving by himself across the city. He was wearing a sharp suit and dark sunglasses, but nothing strange there; it seemed to be his standard daily attire.

He parked on West 19th St., and entered the National Museum of Mexican Art. Well, that was an unexpected destination. On the other hand, it made smart sense. Who would expect to find an ex-military security agent strolling through an art museum? It was a great place for a secret meeting.

Chicago Blue

I hurried up the stairs, into the lobby, and moved quickly to the exhibits (Free admittance! Awesome museum!). I wanted to get ahead of Ralston, so it wouldn't seem like I was tailing him through the museum.

I moved through a few rooms, passing a lit sign that read "Make Tacos Not War," before sitting on a bench in front of a beautiful Flor Gaduño photograph. I thought instantly of my mother, the real Georgette, who had taught Art for so many years until she was forced to resign because of her illness. Some people follow in their parents' footsteps, some run the other way. I'd botched the job completely, following in Dad's footsteps, when really I should have followed in Mom's. I loved art. The Art Institute of Chicago felt like a second home, something I'd never really talked about with my fellow officers on the force. I could just imagine how those conversations would go.

I took a sandwich out of my lunch bag and had eaten half of it when suddenly a docent entered the room. He was a small man, of east Asian descent, in a sharp blue uniform with a name tag that read "Hao." He looked at me, then looked at my sandwich, and shook his head disapprovingly. I looked him square in the eye and shoved the last half of the sandwich completely in my mouth. It was a tight fit, and I had a bit of trouble chewing, but boy did I show him who's boss.

He still didn't say a word. He just looked at me through thick glasses and took up a place against the bare wall by the entryway. It was clear he had decided that he needed to keep an eye on me.

I heard voices, then, coming from the adjacent exhibit space, and turned to see Greg Ralston enter the room, walking hand in hand with Valerie Archer! They were leaning their heads close together, and whispering, but

Chicago Blue

judging from their demeanor they were *not* discussing corporate espionage.

Well, they were both gorgeous, and they worked in the same building. I guess these kinds of relationships happen between coworkers in the workplace. In other workplaces besides my precinct. Or to other people in my precinct, who are not me.

Originally, I would have thought Archer was a bit above Ralston's pay grade, but I was beginning to suspect that his position at Farnham was a bit more convoluted then just being a security guard.

Another couple, retirees by the look of them, entered the room as well, and I returned my attention to the photographs on the wall, keeping my ears focused.

"...you know we can't, yet," Valerie Archer was saying. "Not right now, there is too much going on."

"Oh please," said Ralston roughly, "I'm sure Ferris already knows. I've known him forever, and trust me when I say he keeps tabs on *everyone*, you included."

"Not quite as zen as he appears," said Archer wryly.

"Well, who knows. Maybe he'll become one with the universe soon."

"Greg! Don't even kid about that."

"It would make you the new CEO of Farnham," Ralston said in a teasing voice, but a long silence followed. They were behind me, but I pictured them staring uneasily at each other as the moment stretched. Then Valerie Archer laughed a smooth, honey laugh.

"I don't think that would work out the way you want it to, Sweetie. If Ferris comes to a bad end on your watch as head of security, I would most surely have to fire you."

"I'm ready for the next room, Luis," a woman's loud voice cut in.

"I'm still looking!" shouted the old man, clearly hard of hearing.

Chicago Blue

"Because she's naked," the woman shouted back, yanking Luis by the arm. "You are still looking because she's *naked.*"

Greg and Valerie chuckled to each other, amused by the elderly couple, and started for the archway themselves.

Just then, a sound like a cannon echoed through the room. Instinctively, I rolled off my bench and on to the floor, looking up just in time to see Greg Ralston reach smoothly into his suit coat and pull a revolver from a shoulder holster. Valerie Archer screamed.

From the other side of the room, Hao the docent shouted "GUN!" and leapt at Ralston, grabbing him around the wrist with both hands. I braced myself for gunfire, but it never came.

I assume Hao had intended to wrestle Ralston to the ground and relieve him of his gun, but that of course was not what happened. The man was a mountain, and the docent probably weighed 140 pounds at the most. Greg grabbed him by the back of his uniform and pulled him back and away. Then after looking around the room quickly he put the revolver back in its holster.

"Who are you!" demanded the docent.

"I'm sorry," growled Ralston, though he didn't sound particularly so. "I'm a security specialist. I have a license for this."

"Well, you shouldn't have it in here. You could have killed someone."

"What the hell was that noise?" Ralston said in response.

Hao took a deep breath, I assumed adrenaline was still coursing through his veins.

"It was a foul ball, from Harrison Park next door. Hitting the roof. It happens every once in a while."

152

Chicago Blue

"Are you okay?" asked a voice at my elbow. I turned to see Valerie Archer picking up my broken glasses from the hardwood floor. She reached out a hand to help me up.

"Yeah. Just my pride," I said as I got to my feet. The older couple had fled the room in a panic.

"But your glasses are ruined," she said, holding them up to the light. She seemed suddenly intrigued, and looked at them more closely. "They don't have any magnification."

"Right," I mumbled, taking the glasses from her. "They're just for show."

Archer smiled knowingly, and leaned in toward me.

"I always find museums romantic, too," she whispered. "A great place for a secret meeting."

I gathered up my things. Hao and Ralston were still talking in hushed tones. Hao was clearly still mad at having someone bring a firearm into the museum.

"Yes, well," I said with a bit of sorrow in my voice. "It looks like my date isn't going to show. I've got to get back to work."

"Goodbye," said Archer, and turned back toward Greg Ralston. I felt another pang about having stolen her credit card. Maybe I'd make it up to her someday.

I made my way to the door and out into the sunshine, convinced that Ralston was either deeply on edge about *something*, or that it was time for him to find a new job, maybe collecting stamps or something else that was peaceful and quiet.

26

From a quiet park bench, I called Marty with my new superspy SIM card. I tilted my face up toward the warm spring sun. It was another beautiful day to still be alive.

Marty wanted to talk more about the technology of the SIM than he wanted to talk about Greg Ralston.

"Just please, Marty, can you look into Greg Ralston again. Especially the old stuff. I want to know how he came to be associates with Farnham, and whether or not he had any relationship with Blalock."

Marty grimaced down the line.

"I'll do what I can. Why don't you ask Aldo Frances?"

"Thank you. I would, but everything just seems so insular. I want to keep outside this circle of Farnham and Blalock. Everything seems connected and incestuous, and Aldo is part of that circle. Also, I like him, and I'm worried that he's next on the hit list. I don't want to draw any more attention to him. Dragging him out to the ballgame was a foolish idea. I could have gotten him killed."

"Okay, then, we focus on Ralston."

"For now. The theory I'm working on is that Ralston is trying to get his girlfriend, Valerie Archer, promoted to CEO of Farnham, which means Ferris Farnham is possibly still in danger."

"What about Pershing and this Salerno person?"

"Well, they could be behind it, that's true. Or they could be a red herring, or it could be both things: Pershing destabilizing the telecom industry, Ralston trying to take advantage."

"What about Valerie Archer, or Belinda Blalock?"

"Ack, Marty, I don't know." I paused to consider. "Aldo confirms Belinda's assertion that she doesn't stand to gain anything from Illcom, so I don't see what her motive is."

Chicago Blue

"That's why I like her for it. It's always the ones you don't suspect. In fact, it's almost always the police chief. Have we investigated the police chief yet?"

"No, and we aren't going to."

"And Archer?"

"Well, she has the motive, and the access to technology, but I don't think so. She was really very nice to me at the museum."

Marty snorted. "Kay, come on!"

"I know, it sounds stupid. Sometimes I use my brain, sometimes I use my gut. It's what cops do."

"Yeah, well, I'm a computer scientist, I'll stick to brains. I've got to go. My gut is telling me I'm hungry."

"Okay, buddy. Do me a favor and update Ruby on all this. I'm going to go sit on the Farnham Building for a while and see if I can see anything there."

The Farnham Building was a little out of the heart of things, over in Cabrini-Green, not far from my old station. I knew from researching Farnham that he had picked this area to signal his belief in real urban renewal. Among the office buildings and condos springing up on the site of the old public housing, Farnham planned to build midsize, rent-controlled apartments for Farnham employees. A strange guy, Ferris was. He did everything right on paper: brilliant, virtuous, enlightened; but in person he seemed intensely unlikeable. I didn't know quite what to make of him. Maybe his tie to Blalock was strong because he didn't really have any other friends.

I sat on a bench in Seward Park, where I had a clear view of the front of the building. This made me nervous. I had to keep reminding myself: new hair, new clothes. No one would recognize me.

I was wearing a gray dress skirt and a light blue blouse, with low-heeled shoes that were dressy, but that I could run in if I needed to. I don't think any of my fellow cops had ever seen me in anything other than a uniform, or jeans and a sweatshirt. It was true what Nicholas had said: shifting social class makes you more invisible. Even my captain would probably walk right by me without a second glance.

Nicholas. I spent some time thinking about Nicholas, because stake-outs can cause daydreaming. It's a common side effect.

"Hello, Kay," I heard him say, and then felt a real hand on my arm.

"Christ!" I yelled, leaping up and knocking my water bottle to the ground.

It was him, Nick, in the park, with a steadying hand on my shoulder.

"Whoa, there. Calm down. I'm sorry."

I sat back on the bench, breathing heavily. He sat next to me, real as could be.

"No, I'm sorry. I was distracted, and you just...well, you scared the crap out of me." I straightened my blouse, and put a hand to my head to check that my wig hadn't been dislodged.

"What are you doing here?" I asked him.

"I was just walking by, and I saw you. I'm surprised that you're out in public, even with the disguise. It must be nerve-racking." His voice was smooth and sounded like maple ice cream tasted.

"I guess I *am* a little jumpy," I said. And then giggled. Jumpy was hardly the word.

"I was thinking about you," I said, "and you just appeared. I think I'm going to think about a million dollars now."

He laughed.

"So, what are you doing out here?"

"Staking out the Farnham Building."

"I can see that. Waiting for Ferris Farnham?"

Chicago Blue

"No, Greg Ralston, actually."

"The security chief?"

I narrowed my eyes at him.

"Wait a minute, how do you know about Greg Ralston?"

"I don't really know any—"

"Are you checking up on me?"

"No, I—"

"You are! You're following me." I poked my finger into his chest.

"Uncle Elgort—"

"Doesn't think I can do this on my own? Is that it? Scared little girl?"

He just paused, looking at me until I stopped talking.

"He's worried about you. He, we, don't want to see anything happen to you."

"Why?"

"He feels guilty, of course."

I absorbed this for a minute.

"About Uncle Nick?"

Nicholas sighed.

"It wasn't Uncle Elgort's fault. Not directly. I suppose you realize that I'm named after your Uncle Nick?"

"I suppose I did, on some level. I hadn't really made the connection until the other week at the furniture store. I'm afraid to say I'd kind of forgotten about the Shelby family until all this happened."

"I see." He rubbed his chin with his hand.

"Oh, come on," I said, indignant. "It was ages ago. And Uncle Nick was closer to Eldon than he was to his own brother."

"Of course he was."

"What's that supposed to mean? Because Dad was a cop, and didn't think it looked good to be hanging around with the mob?"

Chicago Blue

"No, of course not."

"Then what?" I searched his face, which had an incredulous look on it.

"Your dad never told you?"

"My dad's been dead for twelve years!"

"Eldon and Nick were more than close, they were a couple."

"A—"

"Exactly. They tried to keep it quiet, but Uncle Elgort figured it out. And, for the record, he was fine with it. Some of his associates weren't, though."

"The explosion..." my mouth was hanging open in astonishment.

"Exactly. Uncle Elgort has always assumed it was in retaliation for something, or just for being gay. Anyway, he's always blamed himself for not being able to protect them."

I was stunned. Not by their relationship, that was no big deal, though maybe if you are in organized crime there's still some lingering prejudices. No, I was stunned that for all this time, I had believed that Uncle Nick died in a gas explosion. That it was an accident.

I thought about the old man, Uncle Elgort. When you're the head of a crime syndicate, and somebody blows up your son, it's inevitable that you think it's all your fault. Even if Eldon and Nick had been into some bad stuff, Elgort would argue they were only in that business because of him.

"You still here?" asked Nick.

"Huh? Oh, yeah. Sorry, I do that sometimes." I turned and looked at him on the bench next to me, and something stirred within me. I was starting to really like this guy. "Would you like to get dinner, later?"

His eyebrows shot up.

"Are you asking me out?"

Chicago Blue

"Umm...yeah?" It honestly didn't seem that strange to me. "We aren't actually cousins or anything, you know. If you're not interested, fine, I just felt..."

"What?"

"I don't know. I felt like we were connecting."

He turned toward me.

"Actually, it seems like we've mostly been bickering."

"Exactly," I countered.

He sighed. It was not a sigh of deep emotional infatuation. It was the kind of sigh you give a misbehaving toddler.

"Or not," I said hastily, and began to gather my stuff.

"It's not that, Kay," he said gently. "It's just, aren't you a little busy right now?"

"There's some downtime, you know. Sitting on benches. Sitting in cars." I put my water bottle back in my shoulder bag. "There's a lot of sitting. Plus, you're following me around anyway, aren't you?"

"Look, Kay. I like you, I really do." His eyes were big and brown. I hated getting dumped before I even got going. Especially by someone with eyes like that. And hands.

"But..."

"But I'm not going to get entangled with you while this is all going on. You've got to be on your game all the time. This is urgent."

"That's why I brought it up now," I pressed on. "I could be dead next week. Hell, I could be dead or in jail tomorrow, and then I would have missed my chance."

"Be that as it may," he began.

"Be that as it may?" I interrupted him.

"What?"

I started to laugh. "You just 'Be that as it may'ed me."

He smiled. "Sometimes I sound like an old man."

"Old woman."

Chicago Blue

"Okay. But my point is the same. If you clear your name and solve this, I'll take you to The Drake for the best dinner of your life."

"Not The Drake."

"What's wrong with The Drake?"

"Long story, which you'll never hear if you wait until I'm dead!"

"I'll have to take my chances." He touched my shoulder gently. "Be careful, Kay," he said, and turned and walked away.

I stood watching him go, fantasizing about that dinner, and after dinner, and after that. However, before my fantasy got too far along, I was snapped back to reality when Greg Ralston exited the building across the street. I jumped up, tossed my Tabaq lunch wrapper in the garbage can, and headed off in pursuit.

27

He was on foot, so I followed on foot, staying well back, though he seemed focused on where he was heading. He barely looked up or around.

I needed to see Ralston interact directly with someone, anyone, who might be masterminding this: Salerno, Watkins, or someone else from Pershing. Or like I said, maybe *he* was masterminding it, in which case I needed to see him do something mastermindful. Something I could take to the police.

I followed him around the corner to La Salle and then right on to Goethe. He seemed to be heading towards the lake, likely to one of the office buildings there, but who knows? It occurred to me for the hundredth time that I really hadn't done my homework. Who was Ralston, really? I needed a researcher on my team, and not just a hacker like Marty. I needed to take the time to know the people I was up against, so I wouldn't keep making the same stupid mistakes.

Face it, I was an amateur. An amateur spy. That's what my biography would be called: *Kay Riley, the Amateur Spy*. With any luck, I'd get a documentary on the History Channel. What's-her-name from *Game of Thrones* would play me during the staged reenactments. Ygritte.

They'd have to be staged re-enactments, because of course I'd be dead. Because I suck at this. Nothing but luck and some shenanigans had gotten me this far. And a little help from my friends. Everything was just moving too fast. I vowed that after today, I would slow it down, create a strategic plan, and execute it. Maybe with a PowerPoint presentation. And if that didn't work, I'd get out of town and out of the country. You don't need that much money to live in Central America, do you? The sun

Chicago Blue

would be a problem. My skin just doesn't tan. How about Saskatchewan?

Up ahead, Ralston turned right and cut through Goudy Square Park, a little playground that I knew from my patrols; teenagers like to hang out there after dark and do the things that teenagers do. A flash of the blues usually got them to move along, without me ever getting out of the cruiser. I followed him into the park.

As I was passing beneath the trees I heard—felt, really—a whooshing sound behind me as something dropped from above. I spun, forearm up and fist clenched, miraculously making contact. Something, maybe a gun, clattered to the cement walkway.

A flat hand struck me in the chest, and I staggered back several paces, struggling to keep my breath moving in and out. The Pakastani food in my stomach gurgled, but stayed put.

In front of me stood Selena Salerno, laughing. She was wearing black boots, with tight red leather pants. Her long brown hair was in a ponytail, and she wore a fitted, short-waisted black jacket. I glanced quickly to the side to see a black plastic box shattered on the ground. It had a velco strap.

"That's my taser!" I gasped, regaining my breath.

"You shouldn't leave your things lying around," she laughed. She spoke with a delightful accent.

"Did you kill Alan Watkins?"

She scowled. "I don't kill people," she said.

Well, that was encouraging, at least.

I looked quickly around, but my options were terrible. Ralston was nowhere to be seen. I doubted I could outrun Salerno, and the odds of beating her in a fight only seemed about fifty-fifty. She was in incredible shape, but I had been training a lot, and felt pretty good about my rudimentary taekwondo. I'd learned it in police training a decade ago, but I remembered most of it.

I could scream for help, but I was a wanted fugitive, and besides, the playground was deserted. Where were all the kids? The nannies? It was the middle of the afternoon, for crying out loud.

"So, red's the color today, huh? Really blends in."

"*You* didn't see me coming."

I ignored that.

"Just needed a change of pace?"

Salerno laughed again. "Actually, Riley, you're exactly right. Sometimes the white suit is out of the question. It's refreshing to be working with another woman. I feel like we understand each other."

"Nice jacket," I said, continuing to stall while I waited for a plan to come to me.

"Sometimes I need pockets," she shrugged.

"But you didn't the other day, when you were stealing corporate secrets from Ferris Farnham."

"Oh, boohoo." She tossed back her ponytail. "Poor Ferris Farnham. He thought he was going to control Illcom, but he was wrong. He's a big baby."

I edged slightly away, toward the jungle gym, but she matched me step for step, smiling like the Cheshire Cat the whole way.

"What was that document, anyway," I asked, offhandedly.

"A take-out menu."

She took a step toward me, and I took another step back, into the woodchips, used as cushioning for kids who take a digger off the play structure. I was getting backed up against a wall, here. I had no choice. I was going to have to fight her.

"You're hilarious," I said, and then kicked wood chips at her face, leaping at her with a sliding side kick.

Chicago Blue

Selena Salerno sidestepped like a ballerina, spinning on one strong, perfect leg while bringing the other one through the air so that her booted foot connected with my head.

A white light exploded in my vision and I went down, hard, to the ground. Jesus Christ what had I been thinking? Of course she could fight! She wasn't a gentle dancer. She was a latina ninja, or whatever the Spanish word would be.

I rolled onto my stomach and tried to get to my hands and knees, but my head felt the size and weight of a Mini Cooper, and blood was trickling into my left eye. I tried to wipe it with my left hand, but lost my balance and fell onto my side. I opened my right eye to see her squat down beside me. With a yank, she ripped the long black wig from by head and threw it aside. My glasses were already long gone. I felt her fingers in my red hair, which had grown just long enough for her to grip. Convenient.

"Ah, *si*," she said. "Red Riley, there she is."

"Don't call me that," I mumbled, trying again to get to my hands and knees. She helped me by pulling hard on my hair, dragging me forward until my head clanged against a metal post of the jungle gym, causing the stars to come out again. My vision kept whiting out, making it hard to retaliate as she kicked me in the ribs, rolling me onto my back. She straddled me then, bending down, her face looming and her ponytail falling in my face. She grabbed me under the arms and pulled me up to a sitting position, leaning me back against the metal bars.

She kicked my legs apart, wider, until I heard and felt my skirt rip, and then she knelt between them, her face just inches from mine. She ran her fingers through my hair again.

Chicago Blue

"I like the real you better," she said. I could only groan as my head lolled to the side.

She reached into her pocket and took out something big and round that glinted in the sun. Oh great, I thought through a haze of pain and blood, I was going to be handcuffed, again. She'd leave me here, chained to the jungle gym without my disguise, for the police to find me. Well, it was better than being killed, I supposed.

Salerno stood and walked away, out of the park, looking back once to blow me a kiss, her boots clacking on the cement.

I looked down at my wrist, and realized I had been wrong. It wasn't handcuffs. It was worse.

On my left wrist was a wide, gleaming copper bracelet, with a green light glowing in the center like a precious emerald.

She had turned me into a bomb.

28

I was a bomb. The idea just kept pounding through my head. I struggled up to my knees and looked again at the solid green light on the bracelet. I was a bomb.

I searched the ground around me. The eyeglasses were crushed, and the wig was useless—snarled and full of woodchips. I crawled over to my shoulder bag and found some tissues that I could use to wipe the blood out of my eye. It seemed to be coming from the upper left of my forehead. I found some old napkins and held them tightly to the spot. My head spun.

I was a bomb.

I looked more closely at the bracelet. It was thick and clunky, presumably full of some kind of explosive, or maybe it was made out of explosive. I didn't know. It had a hinge, but no clasp. It must slot into itself and lock shut. There was no way to open it. My breathing wasn't getting any calmer. My blood was pounding. The only other notable feature was a small jack, like for a pair of earphones.

I was rooting in my bag for more napkins when a phone rang loudly, right behind me. I screamed out loud and whirled to find no one there, but resting on a nearby seesaw was a black flip phone. As I stared at it, it rang again. I didn't scream this time, but I still jumped about a foot.

It wasn't my phone. Mine was still in my shoulder bag. But it had to be for me. There's no way some soccer mom just happened to leave her phone behind, and it just happened to ring right at the height of my crisis. Besides, nobody used old phones like that anymore. Selena Salerno had left it for me.

The phone rang again as I moved cautiously toward it. Still holding the napkins to my head, I reached down with my other hand and picked up the phone, flipping it open with one hand.

"Hello?" I said, expecting to hear her accented voice.

"Don't hang up, Officer Riley!" said a computerized voice.

I hung up. What the hell was going on? I thought I was being so careful, running around the city with my sexy clothes and my dark hair, but somebody had known where I was all along, and what I was up to.

The phone rang again. And rang. I just stared at it until, all of a sudden, the green light on the bracelet turned yellow. I answered the phone in a panic.

"Okay, okay, okay!" I spat into the phone. "I'm here, okay. I get it."

The yellow light turned back to green, a color I've always loved. Clearly the person on the phone could control the bracelet.

"That's better, Officer Riley," said the monotone robot voice.

"Who the hell ar—"

"Please don't talk, Riley. Just listen."

I bit my tongue, spinning in a circle to see if anyone was watching me, but they could be anywhere. Anywhere on the planet. Using me as a bomb.

"What?" I said back into the phone. "Sorry, I missed that part, I was distracted figuring out how I'm going to find you and rip your goddamn heart out of your chest!"

"Now, now. Remember. I talk, you listen. First," the voice continued, "you are to make NO phone calls on this phone, or on your other phone. We are watching, and we are listening. We will know."

"Is that the royal we, or are there a bunch of you cowardly assholes?" I kicked the seesaw in anger. It didn't do much good.

Chicago Blue

"Enough. It's time to get moving. You are going to go back the way you came, and you are going to meet with Ferris Farnham."

"So you can use me as a bomb, to blow him up? I was there the last time, you know. Carter Blalock didn't follow your plan. He blew himself up instead. What makes you think I won't do the same thing? You're going to kill me anyway, right?"

"I have no intention of killing you, unless you fail to follow my directions. Do as you're told," the voice intoned without inflection, "and the bracelet will fall off and you can go back to being a fugitive from justice. You might want to consider a change of venue."

"This is my goddam city."

"Suit yourself, stubborn woman. Though I suppose that is why you are still alive."

"Damn right!"

"For now," said the voice, and the bracelet light turned yellow for a brief second, then back to green. A warning.

"Okay, okay," I said. It was difficult to argue with someone who never raised their voice or got angry. "I'll do it."

"Of course you will."

"If you're not intending to blow me up, what are you sending me to Farnham for?"

"You are simply a courier. He is going to give something to you, and you are going to deliver it where I tell you to. After that, you will be free to go."

I didn't believe that for a minute.

"What am I picking up?"

"Five million dollars."

Woah.

"Alrighty, then," I said nonchalantly. "What do I do once I get to the building. I'm a bit of a wanted woman."

Chicago Blue

"Don't worry, just keep your head down. Put on a hat, I believe you have one in your bag. Greg Ralston will meet you at the front door. They are expecting you."

Ralston, again!

"Is this you, Greg Ralston?" I asked suspiciously.

The computer voice laughed, or at least said "ha ha ha." It wasn't very convincing. "We've met twice, Ralston," I said into the phone, "and you had no idea who I was."

"You do not know me, Riley. Mr. Ralston is acting on Ferris's behalf, and he will make sure you get to the top floor safely, and back out of the building as well."

"But—"

"No more, now. Do as you're told. You are being watched. If you disobey, you will be eliminated and I will simply use someone else, like Ms. Martynek, or her nephew." The phone went dead.

Damn. Damn!

I started moving out of the park and back toward the Farnham Building. I pulled my Cubs hat out and put it gently on my head, using it to hold the napkins against the gash in my forehead. I had about six blocks to figure out a plan to get out of this, protect my friends, and solve the mystery.

How hard could that be?

29

See? Only took me two blocks to solve the mystery and formulate my plan. I'd need to go through with the pick-up to confirm my hunch, though.

Meanwhile, I looked up ahead and across the street, my eyes seeking my target, and there it was: an old Jewel Osco drugstore. I crossed the street and made my way in the front door.

Two things happened immediately. The light on the bracelet turned yellow, and the flip phone rang.

"What are you doing, Riley?" the computer voice said, actually sounding a bit alarmed, as far as soulless machines go.

"I'm bleeding all over the place."

"Return to the street."

"No, I can't see anything. Your chupacabra split my forehead open and I'm all out of napkins. I'm going to buy some gauze and tape and take it to the bathroom."

"We don't have time for this," said the voice.

"Then blow me up, hotshot," I said levelly.

There was silence for a long moment, during which I thought I might pee myself in fear. Finally, the voice spoke again.

"We are watching the entrances."

"Gotchya."

"We are monitoring the phones."

"Yup."

"You will not talk to the cashier, or indicate in any way that you need help."

I looked up at the cashier, who had been staring openmouthed at me since I walked in. Was it the blood? Or was it the generous amount of thigh that was protruding from my ripped skirt? Perhaps saying 'blow me' into the phone was conveying the wrong image. I smiled at him and started down the first aid aisle.

"Okay, Hal," I said into the phone, "and don't forget, there's a window in the women's bathroom. You'd better have Simone Biles cover the back alley."

"If you are not back on the sidewalk in five minutes, I will blow you and the entire drugstore to very small pieces." He hung up.

"Okay," I said brightly into the phone. "See you later, honey!" I picked up the bandages I needed and headed for the back, quickly. I didn't have much time.

I used to come into this store frequently, to get a snack when I was on patrol, back when I ate candy, which I absolutely do NOT do anymore. Especially peanut butter cups. Sure enough, at the back of the store, next to the bathrooms, was an old pay phone. Maybe the last one in this part of the city.

I rushed to it and threw down my bag, rummaging for some quarters. I called Ruby and told her everything in a rush, hoping she heard at least half of what I was saying and what I was asking her to do.

I hung up while she was in midsentence, not really giving her a chance to object, and rushed into the bathroom. I removed my hat and the bloody napkins, washed out the nasty looking cut, taped some clean gauze over it. I washed the dirt and the remaining makeup off my face, and stared at myself for a long moment in the mirror. I was surprised to see that I looked more angry than afraid. Because I certainly felt afraid.

Okay, angry was good. I could work with that. I didn't want to wear the hat anymore, because my head was aching so badly, and to some extent, I felt ready to be myself again, and didn't like all this hiding. On the other hand, I realized that if I was detained by the police,

Chicago Blue

blowing me up would be the easiest solution for this bastard.

So I put the Cubbies hat on, grabbed my bag, and exited the drugstore, turning again toward the Farnham Building. I must have been convincing, because the yellow light turned back to green.

My eyes roved back and forth, both sides of the street, but I didn't see anyone watching or following me. They were *really* good. Nor did I see any police.

Two more minutes, and I walked through the revolving door into the eight-story atrium of the Farnham Building, my eyes drawn inevitably up up up to the magnificent ceiling.

"Miss Riley?"

I jumped, and brought my gaze down to the strong, dark face of Greg Ralston.

"I've been waiting for you," he said.

30

Once again, I was standing next to Greg Ralston in the Farnham elevator. I was beginning to hate this building. I sang "There's a bright golden haze on the meadow..." and then stopped.

Ralston turned his startling dark eyes and matching scowl on me. I couldn't tell if it was in recognition, or if he was just an ornery bastard who didn't enjoy a good musical.

"Greg, do you ever take Valerie out to the Goodman to see a play?" I don't know what was wrong with me, blood loss maybe, or gallows humor. Suddenly everything was funny, and I couldn't help pushing his buttons.

He was less cheerful about it. He grabbed my upper arm, hard, and turned to put his face right in mine.

"I don't know what you're playing at," he growled at me.

"Is Mexican art your favorite? Or was that Valerie's choice?"

That did it. He pushed me back against the elevator wall, his outstretched right hand pushing firmly into my chest, his left hand raised as if to strike me.

I raised my hand up between us.

"Look at this, Ralston." His eyes were drawn instantly to the bracelet.

"You know what this is. Carter Blalock showed you one just like it when he came here that night. He asked you to go get help. And maybe you did, maybe you ran to call Aldo Frances, the smartest person you could think of.

"Or maybe you didn't call anyone, because you knew that if Blalock and Farnham died, your girlfriend would find herself in a much more powerful position.

"But you didn't call the police. Some receptionist working late called us. And then it was too late."

177

Chicago Blue

His hand against my chest didn't waver or lighten its pressure.

"We're going up there to threaten Farnham, and you are either a part of it, or you aren't. And if you're not, you can't stop it. If you didn't know you were a part of it, then maybe somebody is using you. Someone you trust."

He pushed a little harder on my chest. His outspread fingers spanned the entire distance between my shoulders. His eyes were glowing with anger.

Just then the elevator dinged. We had reached the 25th floor. Ralston pulled back and dropped his arm, turning quickly and yanking me from the elevator. He dragged me across the reception area toward Farnham's office, but he kept glancing over his shoulder toward Archer's door.

"Hi, Janice," I said brightly, waving as we passed the desk. The receptionist looked at me strangely, but didn't respond. Ralston put one huge hand on the back of my neck to steer me in the direction he wanted to go, knocking my hat off in the process. I didn't try and go back for it. The time for disguises was over.

Inside Farnham's office, things didn't seem very zen, though the little buddhist shrine was still in the corner. Farnham was standing near his desk, and Valerie Archer was leaning with her back against the plate glass window. They had clearly been having a heated discussion, and had retreated to their respective corners just before we entered.

As I was frog-marched to the center of the room, I couldn't help but glance up at the ceiling. Was the marvelous Ms. Salerno crouched up there, listening to every word? Probably not, as she certainly knows I could explode at any moment. Still, she could have planted a camera or microphone last time she was scurrying about up there. It would be best to be careful what I said.

Chicago Blue

"Easy, Greg," Farnham said, when he saw the way Ralston was hauling me around. Ralston let me go. He glanced at Valerie and then back at Farnham. Was it possible that Ferris didn't know about the two of them? What a moron.

"You can go now, Greg."

Ralston didn't move.

"She's wearing an explosive device," he told Farnham in a level voice. Across the room, Archer gasped.

"Like Carter?" asked Farnham, but he didn't move.

"Exactly. And she doesn't have control over it," he added. "And, she's insane."

I puckered my lips and blew him a kiss, then began to walk toward the filing cabinets.

"Don't move," Ralston threatened.

"Or...?" I asked.

"I'm pretty sure I can break a few bones without setting the bomb off," Ralston retorted.

"Greg!" It was Valerie Archer, her delicate sensibilities shocked.

"You can go, Greg," repeated Farnham. "And take Janice downstairs with you. You'd better clear the 24th floor as well, just to be safe."

"I think Miss Archer should come as well," Ralston said.

"There are reasons she needs to stay," Farnham said, without taking his eyes of Ralston. "It's going to be fine, Greg."

I looked at Valerie Archer, who looked like she would just as soon leave with Ralston. For a while, she had been on my suspects list, although when I got a chance to be up close to her at the museum I crossed her off. My intuition said she wasn't a killer. And, if she *were* the villain, and was standing there in the room as the payoff went down, she was way out of my league. That would be one stone cold move.

"It's going to be fine, Greg," she said, unwittingly parroting what Farnham had just said.

Ralston balled up his fists. If this were a cartoon, there would be steam coming out of his ears. And everything would be funnier.

"Go clear the people out, Greg," Valerie said calmly. "Just in case."

Greg Ralston turned without a word and left the office.

"Bye, Greg!" I called to him as the door was closing. I turned to look at Archer. "He's a real sweetheart."

"Officer Riley," said Farnham, cutting me off. "You seem awfully relaxed considering the situation."

"Well, life moves pretty fast. If you don't stop and look around once in a while, you could miss it."

"You're hilarious," said Farnham.

"Oh, I'm sorry," I said, feigning innocence. "Heard that one before?"

"Greg was right about you," he said. "You're insane. But Aldo was right about you, too. He said you were tenacious, and inventive."

"You talked with Aldo Frances?" I asked, dropping my act for a minute.

"Yes," said Farnham, and sat on the edge of his desk. "As you probably know by now, Carter and I were closer friends than we let on, and we'd both known Aldo a long time. In one way or another, he's responsible for most of the technology breakthroughs that we have depended on over the last twenty years. He was concerned that an outside company was trying to destroy us both."

"Pershing."

"That's right."

Chicago Blue

I glanced at the ceiling. "I've met some of their people," I said with a grimace.

"He also said he was sorry that you got drawn into this, and I must add, so am I."

"Me too," said Valerie Archer. I looked again at her. I could see sweat glistening on her forehead and her upper lip, and her chest was rising and falling noticeably with her breath.

"Does she really need to be here?" I asked Farnham. "In case, you know..." I held up my wrist.

"This is about the future of the company," said Farnham. "A company she might one day run. She needs to know what it takes to be a leader."

"Wow," I said, drawing the vowel out for a long three seconds. "I was starting to like you, but turns out you are a real dick." I turned back to Archer. "You know he had a stock deal with Blalock? If anything happened to Farnham, and vice versa. You'd never have become CEO."

"We were just having that discussion when you came in," said Archer, and her voice had a frosty touch to it.

All three of us jumped a foot when the flip phone rang. I fumbled it out of my pocket and it dropped onto the rug. I stooped to pick it up.

"Oh oh, it's Dad," I quipped. "We must have missed curfew."

I opened the phone and pushed a button.

"Go for Riley, big daddy. You're on speaker phone."

"You should have left by now," said the droning computer voice. "Is there a problem?"

"No problem, we just got caught up chatting, is all."

"Yes, I see Miss Archer is there with you, looking lovely as always." Valerie's eyes opened in alarm, she turned to the window, and then backed away from the glass as quickly as she could. The voice spoke again.

"Do you have the money?"

181

Chicago Blue

I raised my eyebrows at Ferris Farnham, though it made the cut on my head hurt.

"I have it," said Farnham loudly. He opened a cabinet and pulled out a large black duffel bag. He set it on the desk and unzipped it. I looked in and saw an outrageous number of one hundred dollar bills, banded in stacks of ten thousand dollars.

"Wow." No sarcasm that time. That was an impressive amount of money.

"Is it untraceable?" asked the voice.

"How should I know?" I asked with exasperation. "I'm not a bank teller."

"It's fine," cut in Farnham. "It's everything you asked for. Now where is the document?"

"You'll get it, after Riley is safely out of the building."

Farnham's face grew red.

"That was *not* the deal."

"And yet," said the voice on the phone, "you are standing next to a bomb. I have changed the arrangement. The five million dollars is now for your life, and the life of Miss Archer."

I hefted the bag onto my shoulder, it must have weighed about eighty pounds, and was almost as large as I was. I staggered.

"This is going to be inconspicuous," I said wryly. "What's going to keep them from just following me down the street?"

"A good question," the voice responded, and a second later there was a sudden cracking sound from the window. Valerie shrieked as one of the pictures on Farnham's bookshelf exploded with a shattering of glass. I swiveled back to the floor to ceiling window to see a hole the size of a marble, with a corona of cracks around it.

"As you can see," said the voice from the phone, "I have covered my bases. Being a criminal mastermind is actually quite fun. Nobody except Riley leaves the office or even moves a muscle until she is out of the building, and has delivered the bag to me."

Farnham was apoplectic by this point.

"Who the hell are you? Is this how you do business?"

The voice chuckled. "It's all business, is it Mr. Farnham? And how about you, Miss Riley, the police officer. Have you solved the crime?"

I looked down at the phone in my hand.

"No," I admitted, "but I've got it narrowed down."

"Oh, please, do go ahead."

I put down the heavy bag.

"Valerie Archer, Arthur Vincente or Aldo Frances for greed, as each would move up if their bosses died, but only if they *both* died because of the stock agreement. Someone from Pershing for the same reasons. Ralston to move forward the career of Valerie Archer"—Farnham raised his eyebrows in surprise at this, and Archer looked down at her feet—"or Maria Vincente for revenge, or Belinda Blalock for being cut out. The voice modulator means we don't even know if you're a man or a woman. Or it could be some unrelated combination, one party after the document, only after Blalock's death at the hands of another party."

"Congratulations, Riley, you have just accused almost everyone involved."

"I'm pretty sure it wasn't Janice, the receptionist, but other than that, yeah, I suck at this."

The voice laughed its metallic ha ha ha.

"On the other hand," I added in my defense. "I've been kind of busy trying not to get killed for the last two months."

"Enough," said the voice. "Miss Riley, I want you and the bag of money back on the sidewalk and heading east in five minutes."

Chicago Blue

"What about us?" demanded Farnham.

"You will sit tight in your office for one hour, and maybe I won't shoot you, or use this rocket launcher I brought with me to destroy the entire 25th floor."

Woah. Could be a bluff, but then again, the preparation on the part of this guy, or gal, had been outstanding.

"Okay, Dad, over and out," I said, and I closed the phone and slipped it in my shoulder bag. I hefted the duffel again and put it over my other shoulder. Damn, it was heavy. I was going to look like a stumbling fool walking down the street this way.

"You can't leave," said Valerie Archer, coming forward to put her hand on my shoulder. "He's going to kill you."

I lifted my hand up to show the big bracelet attached to my wrist.

"I'm afraid I don't have much choice." I leaned close to her and whispered, "I didn't *really* suspect you," and smiled. I moved to the door, turning back to Farnham.

"Ferris," I said, "you're my hero." And I left.

31

I stepped out into sunshine; it must have been right around 5 PM, and the light was slanting down between the buildings. I started north on Orleans St., sweeping my vision left and right, looking for people looking for me. I figured the phone would ring any minute, and I was right. I had to stop and put the duffel bag down to answer the phone.

"Giordano's Pizza," I said into the receiver.

"Now is not the time for humor, Miss Riley."

"Well, I haven't got that much time left, so... where am I going?"

"Stanton Park, do you know it?"

"Of course I know it, I'm a cop."

"Get moving."

"I've got to hang up the phone. I can't hold it and this bag at the same time, it's dislocating my shoulder."

"Stanton Park, look for Mr. Watkins."

The call terminated. Watkins, oh goody. I hefted the duffle bag over my shoulder and staggered up the street, along Seward Park. Stanton was a few blocks further away. If Watkins was up ahead, that meant Salerno was probably somewhere behind me. I'd rather it was the other way around, as she seemed much more dangerous.

Sweat was pouring into my eyes, more from the fear and adrenaline than from the exertion. This was it, right here and right now, and I was terrified.

I reached the corner of Orleans and Division, the moment of truth. Stanton Park was to the northwest, Ruby and Marty were waiting for me, hopefully, due east.

I paused at the corner, and pulled out both the phones. I took the SIM card out of my smart phone and dropped it on the sidewalk and crushed it with my heel. I hefted the flip phone in my hand for a moment, and then threw it as far as I could into Seward Park. It landed in some bushes.

With that, I hefted the bag over my shoulder and headed east along Division as fast as I could go.

The clock was ticking now. Obviously, the flip phone had some sort of tracking device in it. When it stopped moving they would search the park for me and find only the phone. Hopefully this would be Selena Salerno, and I would lose my tail. If there were more than one of them behind me, or Selena was tracking me by sight instead of GPS, this was going to get a lot harder.

I kept up the pace as best I could, not daring to look over my shoulder until I crossed over to the other side of the street, to the entrance of the Near North Branch Public Library. I couldn't help but glance behind me.

Standing on the corner where I had been moments before, dressed in a black leather motorcycle jacket and matching pants, was Selena. She looked at me with a big smile, and then blew me a kiss.

Damn.

32

I entered the library and quickly moved to the back, where I could see Marty waiting anxiously at a study table, his laptop open and on. He waved at me, but I veered to the side and down an aisle into the reference section. There was a big table holding maps and oversized atlases, and I pulled the duffel bag off my shoulder and stuck it underneath. Wow, it felt good to not be carrying that anymore! I put my shoulder bag underneath as well.

The bag was visible to anyone who came down the aisle, but desperate times call for a penny earned, or something like that.

I raced back around the end of the aisle and careened around another corner to where Marty was waiting.

"Kay," he whispered, "let me see it, quick!" I ignored him and went to the large window that overlooked a back alley. I unlocked the window and pushed it open, then I unclipped the screen and let it fall into the bushes a few feet below, which fortunately made little noise and attracted no attention. I didn't want any innocent librarians being harmed in the making of this feature.

Marty was pulling random wires out of his jacket pocket. "Kay, I need to see the jack, come here."

I rushed to him, but instead of showing him the bracelet I picked up the laptop in one hand and grabbed his arm with the other.

"No time!" I hissed and dragged him across the room and into the men's bathroom.

"What's going on, Kay!" He grabbed the laptop from me like I was maybe not handling it with quite the reverence it deserved.

"Sshh! Get in the stall, quick," I said, and pushed him in, following right behind. I edged around him and then climbed up onto the toilet tank. "Sit!" I commanded, and he turned around and sat. Good dog.

"Oh my god," Marty exclaimed. "Who are we hiding from?"

"Everyone," I hissed. "Just be quiet and—oh crap!"

The green light on my bracelet had just turned yellow.

"Kay, we are running out of time, we've got to get out of—"

Marty's raised voice had muffled the sound of someone entering the bathroom, but now we both heard the footsteps on the hard floor.

"Sir!" a man's voice commanded. "Sir, is there someone in there with you?"

I looked at Marty and made the phone sign with my thumb and pinky against the side of my head.

"No, no. I'm just on the phone."

"Sir, I must insist that you not use the phone in the restroom, or anywhere in the library."

"I'm sorry, it's very important. Bitcoin is skyrocketing and I've got to get this deal done."

"Nevertheless, sir, I must insist!"

Just then the door squeaked open again and shoes clip clopped into the men's room.

"Ma'am!" said the man, aghast. "I must insist that you leave here at once."

"You certainly do insist a lot," said a melodious, familiarly accented voice. Oh boy, this was it. I was outmatched by her before, I doubted I could beat her now while crouched in a bathroom stall. I held my breath.

"I'm just looking for a ring I lost in here last night," she said, and I heard a creak of leather as she knelt to look under the stalls.

"Last night!" the librarian was losing his cool now. "You shouldn't have been in here last night, either."

"I go a lot places I shouldn't," said Selena.

Chicago Blue

Marty took this moment to say loudly into his phone: "No, I can't be there until at least 7 PM, I'm on the other side of town. Just hold the deal for me okay? Goodbye."

"Ma'am, you need to leave here now, or I will call the security guard. You can leave your name at the desk, and if your ring turns up we will contact you." His voice faded as he and Selena left the bathroom, the door swinging closed behind them.

I exhaled, and then nearly giggled. I was sitting on the back of the toilet with a leg draped over each of Marty's shoulders as he sat there facing the stall door. It looked like he had been giving me a piggie-back ride when he had to stop and use the toilet.

"Nice job," I said, and ruffled his hair with my hand.

He stood up and helped me off the toilet.

"What do we do now?"

I held up my wrist to show the yellow light.

"We've got to stall for time. Hopefully Salerno has gone out the window and in the wrong direction, because we have to get over to Ruby fast."

Marty tapped his laptop. "Why aren't we doing it here?

"Yellow light means Plan B. Let's go."

"Wait, what is plan B?"

"B is for bonkers."

"Bonkers?"

"You can say that again, McFly."

We left the money bag where it was. It was possible
Farnham had put some kind of trace in it, and if so,
Watkins or Salerno could shadow Farnham's people when
they came for it. I didn't want to be holding it when that
happened. And, I didn't have time to drag that sucker
around anymore. Money is no good if you're dead.
Ancient Czech saying. Someone would notice the bag
soon, but it would all be over by then. One way or
another.

We went straight out the front door. If she thought I
was still in the library, we were dead for sure, but nothing
happened. We rushed across the street to the parking lot
of the Gold Coast Animal Hospital, and spotted Ruby's
car in the back corner. As we approached, she jumped
out and gave me a tremendous hug.

"What's happening? I've been frantic!" She looked
down at my wrist and saw the giant bracelet, with the
light glowing yellow. "*Kurva!* What do we do now?"

"Plan B, did you bring everything?"

"We can *not* do that. It's ridiculous."

"Kay," Marty interrupted. "Over here, please."

He had set up the computer on the hood of Ruby's
Subaru wagon, and as I stepped over he plugged a wire
from the computer into the jack on the bracelet. The
yellow light on the bracelet flickered for a moment, and
we all held our breath, but we didn't explode, and the
light became solid again, so Marty got to work hacking.

Ruby was standing behind us, her eyes sweeping the
street, her hand in her pocket where, I assumed, she
carried a gun. It was sometimes hard to remember she
had been a street officer once, but she was securing the
scene like a pro.

Chicago Blue

"Talk to me Marty," I said, as his fingers flew across the keyboard.

"Ahh, it's looking a little harder than I thought," he admitted. His brow was furrowed and his mouth was set in a deep frown.

"We are on a schedule here, man."

"I thought we would be doing this when the light was green."

"Yeah, well..."

"Ah," his eyes lit up. "Right, *right*! I should have seen that."

"Martin!" growled Ruby, without turning around.

"I've figured it out," he crowed. I breathed a sigh of relief. "It's going to take about five minutes," he added.

Crap.

"That's way too long," I whined and pounded my fist on the car. "We need to buy some more time."

"What should I do," asked Ruby, ready for business.

"Get the stuff out of the car, and let me borrow your phone."

"No," she said, aghast.

"Just in case. I think I can buy us the time, but we need to be ready. If that light turns red we've only got 10 seconds before it explodes."

Reluctantly, Ruby left her post and went to the hatchback of her car. She removed a bungee cord, a quart of Gatorade, a plastic Osco bag, a mini tape recorder, a roll of duct tape, and the broadsword, then laid the items on the hood of the car.

Despite his concentration on the keyboard, the sword caught Marty's eye and he gave a little cry of surprise.

"That's Gina's! I specifically asked you not to touch that!"

I swallowed a huge gulp of Gatorade. "Sorry, buddy, that's the least of my worries."

Chicago Blue

The realization hit him, and his eyebrows shot up.

"Oh, no. Oh no, no, no you can't do that!"

"If the light turns red, I'm doing it."

"You'll bleed to death."

I pointed to the sign on the side of the building. Gold Coast Animal Hospital. "No I won't."

"It's an *animal hospital!*" Marty protested.

"They do amputations, my neighbor used them last year."

"On dogs! Not people!"

"How much different can it be?"

"You can't."

"I'd rather lose a hand than be dead, but if you hurry up with that thing we won't have to worry about it."

"Right, right," said Marty and turned quickly back to the laptop.

I took another huge swallow of Gatorade, finishing the bottle off. I had to be hydrated.

"I'm going to call Aldo now," I said to them both. Ruby handed me her phone.

"Keep your eye on the bracelet, Ruby. If the light turns red, you hand me the sword and you run. Both of you, run. I'll do the chop, throw the bracelet over the fence, and be right behind you."

"Let me stay and do it."

"It's too dangerous."

"We could do it now," Ruby offered. "While it's still yellow. It would be safer."

She made sense. But I was, after all, very attached to my hand. And I was scared. I felt it would be a lot easier to make that move when the immediate alternative was death.

"No," I decided. "Marty's got this, I know he can do it. This is just the backup plan."

Chicago Blue

Marty made a noise in his throat that could have been described as a whimper, and his fingers seemed to move even faster.

I dialed the phone.

34

"Yes, who is this?"

"Aldo, it's me, Kay Riley."

"Oh, my goodness, Miss Riley. Are you okay? Ferris Farnham just called me."

"I'm okay."

"He called to warn me. He said you might be heading back to Illcom to try and blow me up."

"No, but Selena Salerno tackled me and put an exploding bracelet on me."

"That's what he said. I've been frantic to reach you, but your phone went dead. I can help you!"

"I know, you're the only one that has defused one of these things, but I don't want to put you in danger." I couldn't help but pace back and forth, causing Marty to shoot me a dirty look when I accidentally tugged on the cord attached to the bracelet. I stood still. "The light has turned yellow, Aldo, because I stupidly dropped the phone Selena gave me and it smashed on the sidewalk. I was dragging this stupid heavy bag of money around and I lost my balance. Now she thinks I'm trying to get away. She's going to blow me up!"

"You must come to me at once. I can send a car for you if that helps, so you don't have to carry the money."

"Thank you, Aldo, that would be great."

"You still have the money, yes?"

"Yes, I do. I figure as long as I still have it, she won't detonate the bomb. I've seen one of these things blow up and it would definitely destroy all the cash as well."

"Okay, good. Where are you exactly? I hear dogs barking."

I turned and looked at the animal hospital. I'd been so focused, I hadn't even heard them.

Chicago Blue

"I'm on West Scott; I'm right outside the park where I'm supposed to meet them. There are people with dogs playing in the park."

"Okay, my dear, do not panic. I'll have a car there in two minutes. Don't go into the park."

"But the light is yellow, Aldo."

"Don't worry about that, stay exactly where you are."

He hung up the phone.

I looked at Marty.

"We've got two minutes."

35

"That's going to be close," Marty said in a panicked voice.

"Ruby, get the bungee," I commanded. I got the plastic bag ready, and pulled a long strip of duct tape off the roll and hung it off the side mirror of the car.

Tourniquet, cut, throw, bag over the stump, tape, run to hospital. This could work. And then I'd finally have a nickname besides "Red." If I was lucky, I was going to get one more chance to talk my way out of this. If I wasn't lucky, I was going to be Stumpy.

Ruby tied the bungee cord around my forearm, just above the bracelet. I didn't need to tell her to make it tight; Ruby didn't do things half way. She, too, was sweating, and her face was set in a mask of disbelief and horror. I felt bad. How had we gotten here? Was I sure none of this was my fault, or was there something I could have done along the way to avoid all this?

Ruby pulled me closer to the car, and placed my forearm against the hood so that my elbow and upper arm remained off the car. I looked at my hand, orange in the late afternoon sun, and it already seemed disembodied and alone.

Ruby picked up the sword and hefted it.

"I will do this," she said.

"You need to get out of here!"

"No, this thing is too heavy for you to swing with one hand, and the arc is all wrong."

"Ruby, you can't."

"Almost there," said Marty. "All. Most. There."

And then the phone rang again and I almost dropped it in fright.

"Aldo!" I said in a panicked voice as I answered the phone.

"Where are you?" he demanded.

Chicago Blue

"I'm at the Starbucks across the street. I didn't want to stay on the sidewalk in case Salerno showed up looking for me."

There was a long pause.

"You've known, for how long?"

Damn it. Time to tap dance.

"Quite a while, Aldo. I think since the baseball game."

"So that little speech you gave in Farnham's office was just meant to throw me off?"

"So you *were* listening!"

"Of course I was."

"And Salerno and Watkins work for you."

"Of course they do."

"And Pershing has nothing to do with this."

"Well, they might now, now that both companies are floundering from all this chaos. It's not really my concern anymore."

"Right, I don't get that part." I looked frantically at Marty, but he was so focused on his keyboard that he didn't look up. "If you give the document back to Farnham, you won't be the head of Illcom anymore. Isn't that what you wanted?" Keep him talking. Villains like to monologue, right?

Aldo chuckled.

"Yes, it's funny, isn't it? A case of be careful what you wish for. All those years of creating new and innovative projects, just to watch Carter and Ferris take all the credit, make all the money—"

"You must have done pretty well, yourself, though..."

"Honestly, I made some poor investments. That's what the five million dollars is for. Anyway, turns out being a CEO is not my cup of tea. It's a pain in the ass, actually. No peace and quiet, no chance to get any work done. Just constant inane details."

"You're a big picture guy."

Chicago Blue

"Exactly. So instead of running the businesses, the five million dollars. Two million pays off my debts, the other three million carries me comfortably for the rest of my life."

"You really are a criminal mastermind."

"And you're stalling, Riley. It's time to wrap this up."

Marty popped his head up and smiled, giving me a big thumbs up. Then his computer beeped, and he frowned, and lowered his head again.

"Well, of course I am. Unlike you, I never asked for any of this. But I've been a cop long enough to know that delivering the money to you wouldn't have gotten me out of trouble."

"Are you saying I'm dishonest?"

"Aldo, you just admitted your guilt to me. You never would have done that if you had any intention of letting me live once you had the money."

Ruby had come close to me and leaned her head in so that she could listen in on the conversation. She grimaced when I said this. I don't think she had realized until just now that Plan B was going to be our only way out. We couldn't just give him the money.

"But Ms. Riley, we will keep each other's secret. I will deactivate the bracelet, and give you $500,000 to keep your mouth shut about everything that's happened."

"I'm still the main suspect. I'd go to prison for life."

"I'm sure $500,000 would buy you a trip to a nice quiet island somewhere."

"I'd need like two million for that."

Aldo sighed. "I was hoping to avoid destroying you and the money, because this has been so much work, but if that's what I have to do..."

I tapped the hood of the car with my fingernails to get Marty's attention. He looked up, breathing heavily. I held up one finger and mouthed "one minute" to him. He shook his head in wild panic, and went back to typing.

"But you just said you needed the money for debts!"

"I do, but it doesn't have to be *that* money. I can just do the whole thing again with another bracelet. Another Blalock. Another you. I'm sure Farnham can afford another five million dollars."

At this, Ruby took two steps back, finding a comfortable stance while she hefted the sword to get a feel for it. I knelt next to the front wheel of the car, holding my arm in place with my hand on the hood, so she would have a clean shot at my wrist. I have never seen her look more determined.

"But Aldo—"

"I'm sorry, Miss Riley, you've got nothing left to offer. You yourself admitted that I was never going to let you live. It's time to move on."

"But Aldo—"

The line went dead, and the light on the bracelet turned red.

36

"Ruby, give me the sword!"

"No!"

"Marty, run!"

"No, I've got it!"

"Time's up!" The red light started blinking quickly.

Ruby lifted the sword over her head.

"Brace yourself," she said. And counted aloud: "Three...Two...One!"

She swung downward.

There was a beep as the light turned green and the bracelet sprung open. I pulled away but it was too late.

The pain was excruciating.

The was an explosion of blood.

I passed out.

Chicago Blue

37

And now an update on last week's story, what was originally thought to be a gas explosion on the near west side. Authorities have confirmed an anonymous tip, acquired exclusively by this station, that the explosion was caused by a bomb, located in the apartment of Officer Kay Riley, the notorious fugitive wanted for the bombing of the Illcom and Farnham offices in April.

Our source tells us that police are confirming the death of Riley, based on investigation of the scene, which contained not only remains positively confirmed to be the suspect, but also large amounts of U.S. currency, burnt and destroyed in the blast.

We may never know all the details of the "Red Riley Bombings," as they are being called, as Chicago Police are now describing the case as officially closed.

Actually, I'm not dead. Marty disarmed the bracelet just as Ruby brought the sword down. I yanked my hand back, but she still managed to cut off my pinky and ring finger.

It's laughable that I thought I would do that by myself, then wrap the plastic bag around the stump, then walk myself into the animal hospital. The pain was a white scalpel straight into my brain, and I was out like a light. Fainted dead away. I can't even imagine what it would have felt like to lose the whole hand.

Marty threw up while Ruby wrapped the plastic bag over my hand. When Marty recovered, he picked me up and carried me into the animal hospital. Ruby followed, brandishing her gun. They were not happy to see us, I'm told, but after a minute they set to work with the seriousness of trained professionals. Besides the nonstop yammering of dogs, and the vaguely animal smell, the

Chicago Blue

place seemed clean and efficient. One of the assistants made a quiet move toward the phone, but Ruby stopped her with a raised eyebrow and a wave of the gun.

By this time, I was awake, and another argument with Ruby ensued when I refused to let them reattach the fingers. She blamed the pain killers, but I had a plan already in mind. Plan C. I gave them a false name and then sent Marty to go get the bag of cash and my shoulder bag. The vet on duty sewed up my hand nicely. The cut was right at the base of the fingers, and she had to take a skin graft from the fleshy part of my thumb to do it right. I was impressed. If I ever got a dog, I'd definitely take it there, though the staff would probably run when they saw me coming.

When it was all done, we used the duct tape to tie up the staff and make our escape. I felt pretty bad about that, after the great job they had done stitching me up, but we promised them we would call the police once we were a distance away. We also left them ten grand in cash. The incident never made the papers, so either they didn't recognize me from the news or they thought it better to stay silent.

The next part of the plan was carried out by Ruby and Marty, while I slept the sleep of the drugged in my little college dorm. (We put the sword back right where we found it, after cleaning it, of course.)

Marty reactivated the bracelet. He took one million dollars, the bracelet, my fingers in a baggie, and a few other items to my apartment. I was uneasy about Marty doing fieldwork, but it turned out to be fine. The police were no longer surveilling the place, and there was no sign of Watkins or Salerno, which was good because it took him three trips to move everything he needed from the car to my apartment.

Chicago Blue

I wish I had been there to help. This, more than anything else that happened since that first night in the Farnham Building, marked a point of no return. From tonight forward, Kay Riley would only exist in police files and in the memory of a few people.

Marty tied the bracelet to four cans of gasoline, and put it in my living room on top of the pile of money. He left the fingers in the next room. It was going to be a big explosion, and they needed to be far enough away to escape damage.

Then he pulled the fire alarm to make sure everyone was out of the building, returned to his car a block away, and set off the bracelet bomb.

That's right, I pulled a Peter Pettigrew. The police found the fingers, which matched the prints in my employee file, and they found the shredded remains of a large amount of money. The money was for Aldo's benefit. For me to be safe, he had to assume I was in my apartment, with the money, when our phone conversation ended.

Next up was Ruby's part in the plan, this involved going to the police. I had recorded my conversation with Aldo on Ruby's phone. How could a telecom engineer not realize that he might be recorded during a call? And I thought / was an amateur!

Aldo was arrested. He claimed the recording was a fake, but eventually the police found Alan Watkins, whose boss at the security company had been unaware of the nature of the work he was doing for Frances. He was outraged, and was able to corroborate several of the facts that Ruby had presented.

Oh, how I wish I could have been there to see Frances escorted out of the building, by my own captain, no less. Instead, I watched it on the news, through a haze of opiates, which made me giggle uncontrollably as they put him in the back of a cruiser. It would have been great to be waiting in his house one night, in the dark, for him to come home. I would have liked that, but Plan C, keeping the money, depended on Aldo thinking I was dead. Or, I had to kill *him*, and despite Ruby's worries, I had no intention of becoming a hardened criminal. Criminal yes, hardened no.

Reluctantly, Ruby had also gone to Shelby Furniture to let them know that I was still alive. She thought it better if they, too, thought I was dead, but in the end, she did it for me anyway. Uncle Elgort deserved to know that his help had not been in vain, and Nick needed to know I was alive.

The police exonerated me posthumously. It didn't get much news coverage though, along with Aldo's arrest. Probably at the urging of Ferris Farnham, who simply wanted the entire thing swept under the rug so that his stock price could get back to where it once belonged. My innocence also meant that Ruby and Marty would not be in any trouble for what they had done to aid me.

Nobody could locate Selena Salerno, but that didn't surprise me at all. I was worried about her, which manifested itself in a series of uncomfortable and unsettling dreams. If anyone could see through this whole scheme, it would be her. But would she? And if she did, why should she care? She was a mercenary, and there didn't seem much use in her coming forward and exposing herself to police scrutiny.

So that's it. I chose to stay dead so that I could keep two million dollars. It seemed a fair trade for my old life and two of my fingers.

Two million? Well, I had promised a million to Marty, and I made good on that promise. And I had given Ruby a million as well, so that she could retire in luxury. The

Chicago Blue

last million, sadly, we blew up at my apartment, to make sure the whole thing was *really* convincing.

I'm still recovering from everything that's happened, both emotionally and physically. What do you do with your life when you are a millionaire ghost? I had a few ideas, and they didn't include fancy new cars or jewelry. Cops are supposed to hate vigilantes, but honestly I think many of them would love to see someone step in and do the things they aren't allowed to do. Sidestep the rules for the sake of justice. Chicago has a lot of problems, and many well-meaning people are doing their best to make things better. I'm no Batman, but surely there are some shadowy parts of the city that I can help shine some light on in my own meager way. And I had Ruby to function as my conscience, in case I ever took things too far.

First, however, I needed to learn how to use what remained of my left hand. Then I would talk to Uncle Elgort about learning some of the more nuanced aspects of being a criminal.

In the meantime, I worked out, practiced taekwondo, and caught up on a bunch of reading (with my shiny new Georgette Wrigley library card).

Plus, I was no longer wanted for murder, and I had solved the case, so it looked like Nick and I would finally be going on that date. My career as a cop was over, not to mention my career as a professional piano player, but the future was wide open, and in so many ways, I'd hit the jackpot.

The End

Chicago Blue

Read an excerpt from Diamond White

A Red Riley Adventure #2:

I was at Ruby's place on Nippersink Lake on a frigid December day when Selena Salerno caught up with me. It was a moment I had dreaded for months, hoping it would never happen. Now it had.

When the silent alarm went off, I hoped it was a mistake. A deer, or maybe just the wind blowing so hard it tripped a sensor. The wind chill made it feel like Antarctica outside, and I wasn't that excited about suiting up to trudge the quarter mile to the perimeter. But Marty had assured me that this security system was excellent, and after a few calibrations of the cameras in the beginning, they seemed to be doing their job.

I picked up a walkie-talkie off the kitchen counter.

"El, come in. El, are you reading me?"

There was a long pause, and then a labored voice answered.

"I read you, Kay. How much of this damn wood do I have to chop?"

"How warm do you want to be?"

"I'm actually sweating right now. And my arms are killing me."

"Can you check on camera six? The alarm went off."

"Will do. Can I come in after that?"

"I'm sorry," I said, repeatedly thumbing the button. "You're breaking up."

I turned off the talkie and stepped to the computer desk on the glassed-in porch. I'm pretty sure that before Ruby bought the house the old fisherman who owned it used this area as a fly-tying workbench. There was a battered countertop with a tiny little vice mounted on it, and old pegboard attached to the wall above. The house,

Chicago Blue

for the most part, did not smell like old fish. For the most part. There was still some painting and renovation to do.

It had only been six months since I became a ghost. Someday I'll sell the book and movie rights, and you'll be able to get the whole story. Short version: I was an unassuming Chicago police officer, who was wrongly thought to have been a criminal mastermind determined to bring down two large telecom firms. When the dust settled, I was exonerated, but believed to have been killed in a huge explosion at my apartment.

Only a handful of people knew that I'd survived, and only Ruby and her nephew Marty knew that I had managed to walk off with a few million dollars, which I shared with them. Ruby bought this secluded cabin in the woods, where I spend most of my time training, and Marty leased a large office in downtown Chicago to expand his business, Technology Acquired.

The alarm went off again, making me jump. Silent alarms are only silent at the point of contact. This one was loud in the quiet of the control room. Okay, the back porch. I was still working on all the nomenclature, but "control room" sounded pretty awesome.

I scanned the feed of the six cameras, but all I could see was white. It had snowed hard the previous night and was still snowing lightly. I peered closely at the picture, which was sharp, but small and in black and white. It's possible that I needed reading glasses.

There! Something was moving through the trees, all but invisible in this weather. There it was again. A person, dressed all in white, was moving effortlessly in the deep snow, flitting like a ghost. I leaned closer and closer, until my face was inches from the monitor. The intruder leapt nimbly over a fallen log. They wore a skintight white body suit that covered them from head to toe, with only a small cutout for the face, which was mostly obscured by

Chicago Blue

a pair of tinted goggles, and another cut out for the pony tail.

I leapt back from the screen and gasped. Crap. It could only be one person. The agility, the audacity, and the fashion sense all told me it had to be Salerno. What on Earth had I done to deserve this?

I raced back to the kitchen and grabbed wildly at the walkie-talkie, knocking over and smashing a drinking glass in the process. I frantically pushed the talk button, repeatedly, then realized the power was off.

Hitting the switch, I hissed, "El! El! Park, do you copy? Stand down. Stand down now!" I was going to be the first spy in history to get their sidekick killed in the very first scene. I *knew* I should've have stayed solo. There was no response from the radio. I tried again. "Stand down," I whispered. "In fact, hide. Hide and call Ruby," I added, realizing that the noise from the talkie could attract Salerno's attention.

Thank God I already had my boots on, because those suckers took forever to lace up. I threw on my quilted jacket and ran outside and down the back steps. There was a utility shed between the house and the woods, and I slogged my way to it through the snow. Hanging on the back of the shed were two bright blue kayaks, and I pulled a paddle from one of them. It was rudimentary as far as weapons go, but at least it would be something. Damn, my fingers were already freezing, but my gloves were inside and it was too late to go back; I could hear the soft crunching of someone making their way cautiously through the snow.

I centered myself and controlled my breathing. By holding one hand lightly over my nose and mouth and exhaling slowly, I made sure that my visible breath didn't extend beyond the corner of the shed.

Chicago Blue

I waited. And waited. The steps sounded closer, yet they barely made a sound. For a moment, I panicked. What if it were El sneaking back to the cabin? No, the movement was too quiet, almost indiscernible. In fact, I was just beginning to wonder if I was actually hearing it at all when suddenly, a cloud of vapor drifted past the end of the shed.

I stepped forward, shouting a kiyup, and swung the paddle with both hands. Sure enough, the intruder was right there. She managed to get her forearm up to block the blow, but the force of it sent her into the side of the shed with a thud. Still, she was able to kick her leg out, strong and high, and catch me in the hip as I turned through my swing. The force knocked me sideways onto the ground. The snow was packed here in the middle of the yard, and I purposefully rolled away from her, eight or ten feet, still clutching he paddle, before I jumped back up to a ready position.

She laughed that deep-throated, sultry laugh of hers, pulling off her goggles and smiling at me. It was her alright. She reached up and pulled off the hood, shaking her head and flipping her long brown ponytail from side to side. I took the opportunity to step forward and take a swing at her head, but she saw me coming and side-stepped the paddle.

"Red," she said, still with a smile on her face. "I'm not here to fight you, honestly." She held out her hands, palm up, as if in supplication. I took a step toward her, and with a lightning-fast move she grabbed the end of the paddle and yanked. I was holding it in my left hand, which was missing the ring and pinky fingers, so my grip was poor and she easily snatched the paddle away. I kicked myself for making a rookie mistake, pushing my hair out of my eyes and backing up slowly as she advanced. A few steps more and I passed the large woodchopping block, continuing to backpedal until my lower back hit the neatly stacked woodpile. I looked for the axe but it was nowhere around.

"You've got to be freezing in that outfit," I told her. Delay and diversion were two of my strongest assets, and among the only ones currently at my disposal. "How did you find me?"

"Well, after our incident with the diamonds, it was clear you weren't dead." She began to circle slowly around the chopping stump, and I matched her step-for-step in a slow clockwise circle. "Nice, job, by the way. Pulling that off."

We had circled one and a half times around the stump, both wary.

"Anyway," she continued, "it took some digging to find that your friend has a secluded cottage in the countryside. I thought it was worth a look. *Eschúcha*, I'm only here because I need your help."

That seemed unlikely. It was true that I had helped her, probably even saved her life, but I didn't think she knew about that, what I had done, or even that it was me. Besides, what could she possibly need my help for? She was a one-woman strike force.

"Well, that is interesting—"

I was interrupted by Ellery Park, who had been hiding behind the wood pile the whole time. She popped into view behind Selena, holding the axe backward, gripping the handle just below the blade. Before I could say or do anything she struck Salerno hard across the back of the head with the butt of the axe.

Selena dropped to the ground, groaning. Deep red blood flowed from her head into the white snow as El and I rushed to her side. I scooped up a handful of snow and held it against the back of her head where the gash was. She tried to roll over, but I lightly put my knee on her back, just to keep her in place.

"Woah," said El, somewhat in shock. "Do you think she really wanted your help?"

"I don't know," I said. "Good thing you didn't use the sharp end, or we'd never find out. Let's get her inside."

Need more? Sign up for my newsletter and get a 10,000 word short story:

www.redrileybooks.com

Also By

The Red Riley Adventures:
Chicago Blue
Diamond White
Solid Gold
Agent Orange

The Levelers:
The Grafton Heist
The Train Job

Available wherever ebooks are sold, or at
andrewsauthor.com

Printed in Great Britain
by Amazon